STIT

Cheryl Elaine

Book Designed by Acepub

Dedicated to my Family, friends, and readers, for a lifetime of love and support and for journeying besides me into my realm of imagination.

Marriage is not the bed of roses story books describe. More like a bed of torturous thorns.

And how Emily bled.

Escape seemed an illusion, a mirage of a rocky road between overgrown thickets of despair. Emily couldn't see any light at the end of the tunnel; she wasn't allowed to dream or think for herself and had no alternative other than submitting to his rage.

Andy was a narcissist. Emily could not, and would not, disregard his superiority. Her naivety often clouded her judgment; she was damaged both mentally and physically. Would putting her trust in another lead her to a happy ending?

CONTENTS

CHAPTER 1

Emily Brooke cowered in a corner, her arms wrapped tightly around her waist and her head tucked into her chest, waiting for the assault to finish. *Please stop.* She felt defeated by his strength. Each time his boot struck her, she gritted her teeth through horrendous pain. *I can't take this punishment anymore.* But Emily knew from experience that if she made a single sound or whimper his temper would flare further, and she'd have to endure violent kicks to her tiny, battered body for longer. It was no use . . .

She'd begged him to leave her alone before, but her pleas only warranted his harrowing sniggers and unrelenting temper. All resistance had been stripped from her inner self. Both her body and mind screamed in silent torment—a place she often frequented. Her body displayed waves of twitching tremors that wouldn't still. All she could do was wither and surrender to his cruel punishment. Broken, she whimpered, like a flower in the shade reaching for the sun.

Andy Brooke felt no remorse. Like any thrill-seeker, he was addicted to the excitement of an adrenalin rush, which triggered his inner core. It's what made him tick. He craved the high, to obtain that euphoric feeling; like any junkie, he pushed the boundaries in search of that indispensable feeling. When he let go, he felt on top of the world, the master of his castle, the prince of his domain. How she'd squirm under his reign. Each time he swung a blow, he felt alive, in a state of masculine control. Every muscle quivered with joy and caused his blood to rush, fuelling his excitement. He knew how to treat a woman and that his wife needed direction. Emily was weak. She craved a dominant man, and Andy was the guy to fill those boots.

1

Andy enforced the rules daily, his rules, which were subject to change at the flick of a switch. There were no limits to the depth of his punishment.

Later, when Emily woke, she was immediately engulfed by horrendous pain. At first, she thought she'd gone blind; both her eyes had swollen so much she could hardly open them. She struggled to squint through the narrow gaps, and all she could see was his harrowing shadow standing above her. *Please, no more,* she thought repeatedly. She knew not to speak, though. Before she'd even realised it, Andy had moved. He was now sat on the edge of the bed, mere inches away. Her heart raced and every hair on her body screamed and stood alert, anticipating what was coming next. She could feel her stomach churn and gulped away the bile that rose to the back of her throat. Andy reached out and touched the top of Emily's head, patting her like a tamed pet; she flinched at his movement and squirmed under his touch. Her heart rate amplified to a faster beat; it felt as if it could burst from her chest. Her head thrummed at the temples with a constant, banging, pain that shot through her entire skull. She struggled to still the painful memories; neither could she escape them. *How the hell have I ended up like this?* The memories of the night before were etched in her mind, unshakable and displayed heavily on her body.

Andy spoke as if nothing had happened; he either cared so little for her or he was completely oblivious to her pain. *Who knows what goes on in that twisted head?*

'I'm off to work. You know I'm sorry, don't you? And that I love you?'

Emily nodded her head in agreement. She had no choice, she was too afraid to speak her mind. She craved courage, but the last ounce of backbone she'd had was squashed years ago. *If only I had the strength.* Her voice yelled and rattled in her head like a stone in a metal drum. She wanted to scream out loud, but her fear wouldn't allow it. She felt tethered to his dominance, a slave to his unrelenting need.

Andy's words of love played in her mind. *Love, love…* Andy's love was hideous. If this was love she didn't want it, she didn't like it, and yet she couldn't flee from it either. Emily knew the truth, she had learnt it the hard way. Andy didn't know the meaning of the word 'love'; it was something that lay dormant within him, like a dead, decaying cat.

Emily slowly turned her head away from him and faced the wall. She kept her eyes shut, grimacing in pain as every muscle and joint ached. She tried to keep the tears at bay, but they escaped her swollen eyes and ran down her bruised cheeks. Every tiny movement was excruciating, and her body cried out for sleep; the pain was unbearable— it was hideous and rippled through every defeated limb.

She wasn't a fool; she was broken, physically and mentally. Beyond repair. Her entire body trembled on the outside and on the inside. She'd become a nervous wreck and couldn't think straight anymore. She wasn't allowed to think at all, really—Andy was the master of manipulation. That was as clear as the swollen nose on her face; he'd done a fine job on her again. In her mind she tried desperately to hold onto tiny fragments of her true self, but like with any breaking point, she was lost and couldn't find a way to bring herself back. *When will this stop?* She already knew the answer, although she didn't want to admit it. *It will never stop.*

Andy closed the bedroom door behind him on his way out; he was as regular as clockwork. He wore his smart uniform and his boots were polished. Emily strained to hear the car engine purr as he pulled away. *Thank God he's gone.* She exhaled a heavy breath, even though her ribs hurt, and lay there for some time with her eyes closed. She was surrounded by the darkness of her mind, but this was better than the reality of her truth.

She knew the feeling of relief wouldn't last long and she worried how she was going to get through the day with her body feeling like it had been hit by the impact of a car crash. She couldn't rest; Andy had expectations and she couldn't disobey him. The cost was too high. *Get up, girl, haul that ass out of bed. You've chores to do.*

Emily slowly started to move but it was difficult. She wanted to scream, yell, to sob, to lay there until she felt healed. She had no option; she had to battle through the pain regardless, the chores were calling to her. Tears welled in her eyes. She knew at that moment how Cinderella had felt, under her evil stepmother's rule. *If only this was a fairytale.* She sighed heavily, the list of duties that had to be attended to embedded in her mind. All her body wanted was to lay still and admit defeat. But she couldn't face another beating, not yet, not ever—not that the latter was on the cards.

She lacked the strength to simply sit up, let alone the mettle to battle the soreness. All her strength had evaporated like mist on a hillside; it would never return. She just had to push through the pain. Emily had resigned herself to the fact she had become a shadow of her former self. She felt invisible on so many levels.

She glared through her swollen eyes at the magnolia walls surrounding her and felt some affinity: she was just as plain and washed out. *How has my life come to this?*

Crushed by the assault but propelled by duty to be an obedient wife, Emily struggled painfully to sit upright. Her body screamed in agony; it already showed signs of trauma. She felt numb and helpless, conscious that she'd become utterly weak. She felt small, like a mere blemish on the Earth's surface, but fear willed her on. Emily knew the beating she'd suffered would not be the last. She often thought about running away but couldn't see light at the end of the tunnel. There was no get-out clause for her; she felt trapped, like a timid animal caught in a snare—alone, isolated and humiliated. Her mind ran wild, tormenting her with utter chaos.

This was Emily's truth. Even though she fought her conscience to admit it, this was just another ordinary day in her unforgiving marriage.

CHAPTER 2

The following week passed slowly. Emily's eyes were able to open wide, though they were still heavily bruised; tinged black, purple, yellow and blue. Her aches and pains were still significant, and she grimaced as she pulled the legs of her trousers carefully over her bruised knees before pulling down the sleeves of her baggy sweater; she couldn't stand to look at the unsightly bruising for a moment longer.

She tried to recall every detail of the incident, searching for the trigger—what had she said or done wrong? She already knew the answer. Andy's mood changed like the wind and could be just as unexpected and violent. She tried to recall a time before his mood had changed for the worse, but her memory was blemished with images of his twisted smirk. His cruel words rang in her ears, more prominent than any memory. She didn't recognise her husband anymore. Andy had replaced her with something else he loved unconditionally. His true love came in a bottle.

Emily had heard his excuses time after time, they may as well have been recorded and set to repeat: he had a tough job, the police force was under lots of pressure. He drank for a release—yet another excuse. He didn't think he had a problem, he just liked a drink. Alcohol was his friend, but it was Emily's worst nightmare.

Andy's addiction grew stronger, and so did the frequent beatings. It had been eight years of hell, pain and torment, and Emily quaked when she thought about her future. *That was a joke . . . what future?* The joke was on her. For most of that time Emily hadn't lived, she'd barely existed, permanently in a dream state where she felt that her life wasn't really happening. The future dangled a lifetime guarantee of misery. There was no silver lining or happy ending to grasp onto, or fond memories that outweighed the bad ones. Emily tried to recall the last time she'd stepped from the confinement of their four walls. She hadn't been out of the house for years. She'd become a prisoner in her own home, a slave to Andy's temper. She wasn't religious but, on the off-chance someone was listening, she gave a silent prayer and thanked God that she had been blessed with a back yard—at least it was somewhere to escape to, away from the imposing, continuous walls surrounding her.

Emily often day-dreamed; she yearned for the simple things: the wind in her hair, feeding the ducks in the park, inhaling fresh air on a summer's day in a place full of green trees and budding flowers. Neither could she recall the last time she'd been wined and dined. Watching cooking programmes on TV was the closest she got. They'd sparked her thoughts and she'd fantasise about what it must be like to sit by candlelight eating fine food with good company. *Ha-ha, that was laughable.* Andy was anything but good company. The flowers and rainbows evaporated from her mind, leaving a dark, harrowing void. Andy's boundaries didn't cease; in fact, they were limitless. He owned a mobile phone for work purposes—that's what he said, anyway, that it was important for his job. He gave Emily no explanation as to why she couldn't have one, just that it wasn't allowed. Not that she had anyone to call. A mobile was strictly off limits, and social media was a definite no-no.

The only things Emily had in life were the blows from her husband's fists and boots. She was well acquainted with the latter, the left and right. There had been many a morning when she'd borne the mark of his heavy sole that had been stamped into her skin, like a tattoo. Many mornings she'd see an image in the mirror of a battered body that could have belonged to some crack whore working the streets, but the eyes glaring back at her were her own; she would pinch herself to make sure her sight wasn't deceiving her. Unsurprisingly, Emily had become a nervous wreck. With constantly trembling hands, she resembled a timid mouse scrambling against the street's alley cat. This particular alley cat liked to taunt its prey. Emily was Andy's prey, that had been established on many occasions, and like many a predator he devoured her strength, blow by blow. *This isn't living, it's barely existing.* Emily hated her life, as well as herself.

Later that day, after a mound of household chores, Emily glanced at their wedding photo on the fireplace. Andy towered above her by at least a foot, even though she'd worn heels. His dark, wavy hair was swept back, and he looked deeply in love as he gazed at her. Andy hadn't looked at her that way for so many years it was hard to pinpoint when it had stopped. Andy's new look was rage, and he wore that daily.

Emily recalled watching romantic comedies, reading romance books . . . a time when the world seemed like an adventure. Back then, she'd thought putting on that wedding dress would be the start of her 'happy ever after', and that the rest of her life would be full of joy. Kids, perhaps a dog, too . . . how wrong could she have been? *How blind?*

The word 'marriage' scrambled around her head like a marble in a dish, prompting the thought that marriage should come with a warning sign—maybe even a trial run. For Emily, the ring was non-returnable. Marriage was not all it was made out to be. She wondered who had come up with such a chain-binding idea and if they'd intended it to be a ritual, so binding and miserable. She presumed marriage was a man-made thing; man being the dictator of all things sacred, because she felt no god.

Today, in that instant, the photo made Emily think of her mother, May. Emily wondered if marriage was a case of 'monkey see, monkey do'; her father had been an arsehole and a shitty husband. *But that's another story.* He'd passed away years ago and Emily had never given him a second thought.

May didn't make it to Emily and Andy's wedding, through no fault of her own. At the time, she'd been in a residential care home, and even though she suffered from dementia, her rantings ran through Emily's head: 'He's a bully, that 'un. I don't like him one bit.' Emily had put her mother's outbursts down to her illness, but now she wondered whether her mother had seen from the beginning what Andy was. How she wished she'd taken more notice back then. Emily missed her mum; she felt alone.

Her happy memories were suddenly brought to a halt when she heard Andy's Volvo pull into the driveway. Fear quickened in her heart. Jumping to her feet, Emily anxiously fluffed the cushions on the sofa before running into the kitchen and checking the roast.

Andy worked shifts—as regular as the watch on your wrist. He never had any time off. He wasn't often seen out of uniform and his shiny boots were never off his feet. He even wore his boots to the pub; they may as well have been glued on. Emily didn't know how he managed to work for the police, stinking of booze as he did, with no questions asked. She didn't have the courage to brace that question. Andy took his job seriously—work was his whole life, and she was at the bottom of his list of priorities. He wore that uniform and badge like a second skin—polished and proud, a respectable pillar of the policing community, and yet a different being behind closed doors where his true nature could be free. He was nothing but a control freak and a violent bully. Emily often mapped out escape plans in her mind, yet her cowardly chicken-heart kept her captive.

Emily balanced Andy's dinner plate in her trembling hand as she concentrated on not spilling the lashings of gravy she'd poured over the roast. She set it down in his regular place. She tiptoed around the kitchen, with only the sound of his footsteps for company, and retrieved cutlery which she placed neatly on the table. She then yanked the ring pull of his can of beer while Andy removed his jacket and hung it on the hook behind the door. In his arm he carried the day's newspaper. He sat down at the table and read the sports page first, as he simultaneously stuffed his face. *It's like Groundhog Day.* But this was not Groundhog Day, it was real, a never-ending labyrinth of nightmares with no means of escape. Andy's routine never faltered, it was depressingly predictable; neither did Emily's nervous disposition, which displayed in her trembling hands as she fumbled with her cutlery.

Emily sat opposite him. On the outside she'd learnt how to control her emotions, and therefore appeared calm. On the inside, though: a rush of anxiety, her soul yelling to be free. She averted her eyes from her meal, waiting for his permission to eat, but he was preoccupied, sniggering at the latest headlines. Years ago, such silence had irritated her, but she'd learned from Andy's brutal hands that it was better to keep quiet than say the wrong thing and give him an excuse for his violence. She had learned not to speak unless spoken to. She wouldn't disobey him; her fear wouldn't allow it.

Andy ate like a farmyard pig in a hurry, slurping, glugging and chomping loudly. Within minutes he'd consumed his dinner. He patted his stomach in satisfaction; his mannerisms grated on her. Emily didn't feel that hungry, her appetite had slipped of late; she was satisfied with just a couple of mouthfuls and chewed slowly on a few green beans before placing her hands in her lap. She knew the routine well, she couldn't move from her chair until she'd heard the last glug of his beer—only then could she stand and remove the plates. Conversation or any sign of appreciation was a thing of the past, never mind acknowledgement, not even a simple hello or thank you. Andy slid his empty plate forward. Emily flinched, and her eyes flickered as it scraped across the wooden table-top, then Andy took himself off for a shower.

Emily strained her ears. She could hear Andy whistling as he showered. *What's he so happy about?* She hadn't felt happiness for so long. Her heart sank. Emily stood at the basin, frantically scrubbing at the stains as if washing her own sadness away. She tried to anticipate his next move; she didn't need a crystal ball, it was obvious: either a night in front of the television or an evening at the pub. Emily didn't have the courage to ask questions, she knew better than that; it had become the norm to just follow his lead. She often thought of herself as a donkey being led to water, but this elixir wasn't magical—in fact, it left a sour taste in her mouth. Emily craved simple conversations—any form of comfort—but the truth was she couldn't remember the last time they'd had a discussion or felt any intimacy between them. The only interaction seemed to be when he was upset with her, which was a daily occurrence.

Emily finished her duties with sore fingers and sadness across her face, as though she was a house maid on minimum wage. She still hovered in the kitchen, trying to look busy and wiping down any minute stain—at least then Andy couldn't comment. Forty minutes later, the crunch of his boots ascended down the stairs and he walked out of the door without muttering a single word. She sighed with instant relief, the first breath of untainted air in a home fuelled by fiery tension. Even though he'd gone, she already feared his return.

Finally, she could put her feet up, worn out from her endless to-do list. Andy's tasks could never be questioned;

she'd learned that the hard way. She settled in the armchair in the living room and pulled a woollen blanket over her lap. Andy had moaned about the electricity and gas bills. The previous year he'd tossed her into the back yard when she had only her nightwear and slippers on; his cruel words rattled around her mind. 'I'll show you cold, you ungrateful bitch. I'm the bread winner. I pay the bills while you sit pretty.' The heavy snow hadn't let up for two hours and Emily couldn't find shelter. She'd just stood there, frozen, sobbing; painful pins and needles led to a numbness throughout her body. It had been a bad winter, the worst she'd ever seen, and the house had been freezing cold, but she never complained in Andy's company again. From that day on, she knew not to turn up the heating dial, and that a blanket would have to soothe her blue mottled skin.

Picking up the remote, she turned on the television for company, but she could only concentrate on the clock ticking . . . she was already dreading his return. *If only I could turn back time. I'd do things differently.*

CHAPTER 3

It was a Friday and Emily assumed Andy was out meeting his work colleagues, which was his usual routine. Around 7.30pm he'd leave to meet the lads from the station, arriving home around 11pm. Over the last few months something had changed. Emily didn't know why, but Andy's timing was not as predictable as it had once been; sometimes it was way after midnight, or even the early hours of the morning, when he returned. She wouldn't dare ask where he'd been or what he'd been doing. *Maybe he was called on a job, or someone's sick from work.* Nowadays, he spent most evenings out and fewer sat drinking in-front of the television. It suited her better, if she was honest. The more time they spent apart, the less chance she'd cause him any upset.

He'd seemed more agitated than usual today, but she kept her mouth shut. Curiosity could bring serious repercussions and she didn't want to ignite his fiery temper. She knew something wasn't right—she could feel it in her bones, that he was ready to punish her. She'd felt the vibe before, it was like her insides were screaming in warning. *Was there something I did, or didn't do? Did I miss something? Am I losing my mind?* She talked herself through the chores, the checklist imprinted on her mind. She'd put the rubbish into the correct recycling bin, scrubbed the bathroom until it shone, scoured the kitchen floor by hand, made dinner on time, straightened the cushions with precision and turned down the sheet on the bed. Her cracked skin and sore fingers were a constant reminder of her workload. She wondered if there was a cobweb she'd missed that Andy had spotted. She scanned her surroundings with a keen eye, checking every nook and cranny. Andy wouldn't like it one bit if standards had slipped. Each day she had a strict routine that she always followed. She asked herself many times: *why, if I can straighten out the furnishings with such discipline, why can't I shape myself?* Her thoughts drifted. *Maybe it's just me, I'm not worthy. I asked for it. What am I doing wrong? I'm just a failure.*

She spent several hours analysing herself, trying to remember the young, carefree woman she once was. The rush of freedom, how it felt to wear a permanent smile. Those days were long gone, like a distant memory. That side of her would never resurface, Andy had made sure of that. Routine was the only thing that kept her going. *What's changed, and why?* She wondered if his alcohol misuse had hit another level or reasoned that he could be working on a serious case that was overwhelming him.

She watched the clock turn 11. The apprehension was torturous, and her stomach twisted into knots; she felt like a prisoner counting down on death row. She tried to shake off premonitions of what was to come when he returned. She wasn't physic, she just knew him better than he did himself. She prayed he hadn't had a bad day and hoped the alcohol he'd consumed wouldn't bring forth any repercussions.

Emily's gut instincts were on point, her senses tuned into his. She had felt it in her bones after all. Andy was more than an hour late from his night out with the lads. As she heard him turning the door knob, anxiety made every inch of her skin quiver and she gulped to swallow the bile that had risen in her throat. She fiddled with her hands nervously, her body stiff and her eyes wide. There was a moment of hesitation, and Emily thought she'd misread his mood and that everything was fine, that he'd just take himself up to bed and sleep off the booze. But she was wrong.

It was obvious Andy had been drunk when driving home; she could tell by the sway in his footsteps as he approached. He staggered through the doorway, his boots gleaming but his clothes ruffled. He had a strange smile plastered on his face as he headed towards her. It wasn't an expression he often wore; Emily considered booze to be the reason, but his eyes told a different story. She blinked several times, to check if she was dreaming. It was hard to accept that he was smiling.

A smile didn't seem to fit his face. It wasn't the norm— he only showed anger usually. Emily felt unnerved by his sudden change in his persona, like he'd momentarily been replaced by another. *Is that just wishful thinking?* She couldn't pull her eyes away from the corners of his lips. He smiled in a way that she'd not seen for years. *Maybe there is something different after all. . .*

Deep down in the pit of her stomach she knew the truth. Andy was cruel and sadistic. She already knew where this was going. He hovered inches away from her, his breath stinking of booze and his clothes of stale cigarette smoke. She didn't move. She didn't even bat an eyelid, though inside she felt panic and wanted to run. Fear grounded her. She remained in the armchair as a cold chill ran down her spine. *Relax, don't provoke him.* She willed herself not to flinch.

He stumbled slightly, and his smile amplified into a sarcastic grin. She didn't like it, not one bit. Her subconscious was screaming—beware!

A cold sweat lined her brow. She felt dread wash over her like heavy clouds on a dark and stormy day. She forced the corners of her mouth to form a warm smile; pretence was something she'd become accustomed to. She had to look convincing, even if her trembles were giving her away.

She plucked up a little courage. 'Everything okay?' she asked, a nervous wobble in her throat.

Andy threw back his head and laughed, as if mocking her. 'Just fucking fine.' He smiled again as he held up a wad of money and waved it in the air.

'Where did you get that?' she asked, as though she really was interested in his windfall . . . in *him*. She cursed herself; she shouldn't have said anything. Her words just seemed to irritate him, and questions aggravated a situation.

'Card game,' he snapped.

'Oh.' Emily tried to look pleased for him.

'Is that all you can say: *oh*? Aren't you happy for me?'

'Yes, of course.' Her bottom lip quivered.

'Ungrateful bitch! I clothe you, feed you, put a roof over your fucking head, and you can't even thank me.'

'Thank you.' Emily hung her head, her mind already singing with distress calls.

'I think it's time you played the dutiful wife. You've been lacking in that area. Then you will thank me,' he said, through clenched teeth. Mocking her, his cruel laughter was haunting.

Emily wanted to run. *But where to?* She had nowhere to hide. She was totally alone with no one to rescue her. Her eyes widened with fear; she already knew that her words would not protect her. *Why don't I have the courage or the energy to speak back, to run away from here, to run away from him?* She always did what was expected of her, she nodded her head in submission. *I must play his evil game, even if it destroys me, it's the only way to survive.*

Even though she didn't like where the situation was going, she resigned herself to the fact there was nothing else she could do. There was no alternative. His smile had disintegrated, replaced by an ugly frown, his brow narrowed into a hard line. His rage seemed different. Though she didn't know what to expect, she knew it would be some sort of punishment that she couldn't escape.

She didn't have time to brace herself, everything happened so quickly, Andy sprung forward, his eyes penetrating hers with a dark glare. He grabbed Emily by the roots of her hair and violently yanked her from the armchair. She squealed under his rough touch. With a fistful of her hair between his clenched knuckles, she couldn't escape him; he dragged her up each step of the stairway. She yelped with each tug, but he ignored her desperate pleas. Emily felt that her legs weren't her own; they turned to jelly and her stomach twisted in knots.

He picked her up by the scruff of her nightgown and flung her onto the bed. Instantly, Emily's sobs amplified, and she instinctively pulled her limbs towards her, tight into a ball. The beatings were bad enough, but this was another level—he hadn't touched her this way for years. He came towards her with such savagery, he reminded her of a starving beast, unrelenting and sadistic. Emily tried to scramble towards the bedhead, away from him, trying desperately to put some distance between them, but it was no use. 'No, please don't,' she pleaded, as he gripped her ankles in a vice-like hold.

He yanked her forwards towards him and spread her legs wide. Emily squirmed. He removed one hand to fumble with his zipper, holding her down with the other. Her heart was racing, thumping, almost jumping from her chest. Tears swam in her eyes until her vision blurred. *Please, if there is a god, make him stop!* He perched on his knees between her parted legs and eagerly ripped at her nightdress until it was shredded. Emily didn't feel love; she felt cheap, ashamed, unloved and petrified. All she could do was grit her teeth. Andy's full weight overcame her tiny frame. Her limbs were stiff and rigid.

He entered her with force, pounding away like a jack hammer. His mouth moved from breast to breast as he violently sucked and bit Emily's nipples, bruising the delicate skin around them. She felt his fingers move inside her as well as his cock, as he tried to spread her open even further. He was rough, without any consideration for her— and only interested in fulfilling his sadistic needs. Emily yelped and sobbed whilst Andy grunted on top her. His breathing was heavy, and his breath smelled of stale booze; she swallowed to stop herself from vomiting. She turned her head towards the wall, away from the stench, but it lingered in her nostrils.

Emily watched the clock, focusing on its hands and hoping that the minutes would go faster. For half-an-hour he brutalised her. Eventually, he climbed off and reached into his trouser pocket for a cigarette. Emily lay deathly still on the bed, broken by his violation. Andy left the room, surrounded by a cloud of smoke, without saying a word. The moment he was out of sight Emily sobbed into the pillow, irrevocably damaged.

CHAPTER 4

Four weeks passed. One Tuesday, mid-morning, Emily was once more running through her list of chores. She gazed through the window. There was a little sun, though a brisk wind looked to be getting up. *At least it looks like the rain will hold off. It's a nice day, considering the time of year.*

Tuesday was always bedding day. *At least it gets me outside.* In a way, laundry day was her release; she had an excuse to spend some time in the back yard. She admired her few flowerpots—they showed signs of summer nurture, yet the blooms were fading and losing their colour. The last of their green leaves were beginning to fall. Emily could relate. She thought they were symbolic of her life: colourless and falling, surrounded by dead leaves, left only with the torturous thorns. She wished that the breeze would whisk her away like a leaf on the swirling autumn wind.

She stood for some time, feeling the freshness of the crisp air blowing through her hair. She hoped it would blow the cobwebs from her mind that bound her to this awful life, so she could start over. Her mind drifted off . . . She envisaged wearing ruby slippers whose heels she could click to disappear from there.

She pegged out the washing, humming quietly to the radio playing in the kitchen. An old, familiar tune took her back to her younger days, when she had hopes and dreams for her future. She thought of her old school friends and wondered what they were doing. *Have they got families or high-flying jobs? Are they happy? Do they have the life they dreamed of?* She felt a pang of sadness. None of the things she once hoped and dreamed for were available to her anymore.

Positioning the last peg on her final item, Emily heard the voice of a stranger drifting on the air. She strained to eavesdrop on the conversation. The husky voice came from over the fence. They hadn't had neighbours for more than six months. Curiosity gets the better of her. Straining on her tiptoes to glance over the top of the fence, she sought a face to put to the voice. A thought struck her: *it could be burglars!* She let out a sigh of relief when she saw a man with a demeanour as smooth as his voice. Her eyes scanned him from head to toe in a flash. He had a mobile phone glued to his ear and was dressed in a fine grey suit that looked like it was designer.

He caught a glimpse of her from the corner of his eye and he immediately brought his call to an end. Emily realised she'd been spotted. She felt apprehension and excitement, like a thousand butterflies are fluttering in the pit of her stomach.

'Hi, I'm Donovan.'

His tone was warm and gentle. *How refreshing...* Emily tried to maintain her balance on the end of her toes. Their eyes met and immediately her face flushed; he was dashingly handsome. Emily's eyes lingered upon his a little too long. She took in his rugged, chiselled features. He was tall and lean with thick dark hair and the shadow of a well-trimmed designer beard. She felt flustered and tried to tame the schoolgirl grin on her face; she was a little taken aback by his good looks.

He appeared to be about thirty-five, but he could just as well have been forty-five. She felt he was older than she was, but it was quite hard to tell his age. She tried to reply but her mouth had gone dry and she ended up mumbling like a shy teenager. 'Hi,' she muttered. 'I'm Emily.' She tried to tear her eyes away from him and banish the wicked thoughts that had rushed into her mind. *It's just nice to see a smiling face . . . a beautiful face, no, a handsome face . . .* Her thoughts ran away her, somewhere dreamy where she didn't venture very often. It felt good, she had to admit.

'Nice weather,' he said, making small talk.

'Yes, lovely.' A grin spread across her face. *Oh my god, he's yummy!* Emily gave her head a little shake. She needed to get a grip of herself and still her wandering mind. *What am I doing?!* Emily hadn't spoken to anyone for years, let alone felt such emotion. She could feel her legs turning to jelly, and she suddenly felt awkward and clumsy.

'What's the neighbourhood like?' he asked.

'It's nice,' Emily replied, even though she didn't really know anything about the area, let alone anyone who lived nearby. Her mind suddenly snapped back to reality; she couldn't tell Donovan the truth—that all she knew of were the four walls of her home. Her prison. Or that her husband was a control freak who didn't allow her to go out. Or that she hadn't walked through the neighbourhood or spoken to anyone in the street for many years. In fact, when she really thought about it, it had been at least seven years since she'd last socialised with anyone; so long ago she couldn't really remember—the days and years just seemed to blur into a life sentence. She fumbled with the washing whilst Andy's warning rang like an alarm bell loud and clear in every corner of her mind. He often told her she needed no one except him. She couldn't disobey him by talking with a stranger.

The harrowing truth was that Andy needed her to be there solely for him, exclusive to him only. She'd become his personal punch bag in many ways, more ways than was natural. Andy kept himself to himself and he expected Emily to comply with the same rule; he didn't fraternise with the neighbours or engage in small talk, therefore neither could she. On many occasions he'd said that members of the police force didn't socialise, and neither did their wives—it was an unwritten rule. According to Andy, neighbours had too many skeletons locked away in their closets. The only reason anyone would want to befriend him (or her) would be to fish for information on important cases he was working on. He described the dangers of being married to a member of the police force; friends and acquaintances were just another restriction on his endless 'can't do' list.

But Emily couldn't help herself. Andy was at work. He wouldn't find out that she'd been talking with the new neighbour. She felt the need to fiddle with the items on the line again; she straightened and adjusting the pegs, hovering. An excuse to hear Donovan's heavenly voice. She craved his attention. With his warm expression, good looks and soothing voice, she could look and listen to Donovan all day, if it was possible.

'Maybe I could call round for coffee sometime, get some insight on the place? I saw your husband leave for work earlier, but he'd gone before I had chance to introduce myself.'

Once again, Emily was suddenly thrust back to reality the moment Donovan mentioned the word 'husband'. *What the hell am I thinking? If Andy catches me fraternising, I'll be in so much trouble.* Thoughts of Andy's harsh, unrelenting punishments overshadowed the delightful musings she'd had just moments ago. She felt tremors take over every nerve ending and inch of her skin. Her eyes widened with fear and her happy emotions deflated instantly.

Quickly, she nodded her head, as though agreeing with Donovan's suggestion of popping round for coffee, when in reality she was confirming her own thoughts: talking to him was dangerous. She had to get away from him, hurry herself. With despair written across her face, she gritted her teeth and forced a smile before turning on her heel and running back into the house. Palpitations hammered against her chest wall. She didn't realise how abruptly she'd fled until it was too late, when the door frame vibrated from the impact of her banging it shut behind her. She leant with her back pressed against the glass pane of the door, panting with anxiety. She felt like a fool. Bringing her hands to her face, she sobbed. Tears flooded from her eyes. *What the hell is wrong with me? I'm so lonely. This isn't how I want my life to be . . .*

Donovan was puzzled. He scratched his head, alarmed by Emily's reaction. *Was it something I said?* He pondered what could have prompted her to run like that. *Was I too forward? Or is it because I'm not much of a conversationalist with the ladies?* It had completely thrown him, and it certainly wasn't the introduction he'd hoped for. He peered over the fence for a little longer, confused by the whole scenario. *Maybe she doesn't like coffee?*

Emily mumbled under her breath, 'Christ, Christ, what am I playing at?' She slammed the worktop with her fist before repeatedly hitting herself at the side of her own head. *Andy would surely kill me.* Her mind raced irrationally, full of doubt, self-loathing and fear. . . *What if Andy had walked in at that moment?* She recalled her puppy-dog eyes and wide smile as she'd drooled over Donovan. Andy wouldn't have liked it, and Emily wouldn't have liked her husband's wrath or the pain he would have inflicted. She shouldn't talk to Donovan again. Ever. Not even look in his direction.

Emily knew she had to banish Donovan from her mind, erase him as though she'd never met him. She shouldn't talk to anyone. *What had come over her?* She knew the answer; she was attracted to him. To the fairy-tale; he was a knight in shining armour who could whisk her away from her misery. But real life wasn't a fairy-tale, it was torture at the hands of a villain. *What if Andy finds out? He'll be furious—more than furious. Totally livid.* Emily paced the kitchen floor, almost in a state of hysteria. Eventually, she talked herself down into a calm state. *Andy won't know about it, how could he? He's at work. And I have nothing to hide—it was just hello, for God's sake.* Regardless, somewhere in the back of her mind she feared he'd find out and that she wouldn't be able to escape his punishment.

CHAPTER 5

Thursday evening, before Andy had even showered or shaved, Emily was startled by a knock at the door whilst drying the dishes. It was too late for cold callers and Andy never invited anyone to the house. Tea towel in hand, she answered the door and her jaw instantly dropped. Donovan was on her doorstep. In one hand, he held a bottle of red wine. In the other was a bunch of gas station flowers, which he waved towards her. She refrained from reaching out and taking them. He sported a wide smile was dressed in the same grey suit as before. Shiny black shoes completed the look.

He looks amazing . . . Emily had to reign in her thoughts while trying to tame her shaky legs. 'Thought I'd better introduce myself a little better. Get to know the neighbours!' His gorgeous smile seemed to illuminate the contours of his face. Emily just stared at him in shock. Her mouth was wide open, and a strange feeling shook her body from head to toe. She felt such a rush of blood to her head that she feared she may faint. *What the hell do I tell him? I can't invite him in! He must go before Andy hears him.*

Donovan didn't appear to notice Emily's shock, or how many times she looked over her shoulder. He seemed oblivious to how agitated she was. 'Erm, it's not a good time,' she practically whispered, just as Andy's voice boomed from upstairs.

'If that's the bloody Jehovah's Witnesses, get shut of them!' he yelled.

Emily rushed her words, her cheeks flushing scarlet yet again. 'It's not a good time,' she repeated, her head swirling with thoughts of how Andy would react to their handsome neighbour.

'Really?' Donovan's voice was soothing.

She looked behind her before opening the door a little wider. When she allowed her eyes to lock on his face, she felt lost in his warmth. She took a few seconds to form her next sentence and shook her head repeatedly, desperately hoping Donovan would take the hint. *I need to make him go!*

'I'm really sorry. It isn't a good time.' Emily could feel her blood pumping through her ears as she repeatedly checked over her shoulder that Andy hadn't appeared.

'It never is,' said Donovan, disregarding her words and gently nudging past her. Emily could feel her anxiety rising from the pit of her stomach. She was speechless. She glared at Donovan as he hovered at the bottom of their staircase, his eyes scanning his surroundings. Emily felt the colour drain from her face.

'Nice place,' said Donovan.

Emily's eyes were so wide she had to remind herself to blink. Her stomach churned, and she felt sick. Her head was telling her that Andy would go ape. *He doesn't like visitors, he won't like it.* Her feet felt as heavy as lead boots as she tried to think of what to say to get rid of him. Before she could put her confused brain into gear Andy came thumping down the stairs, two at a time. He came to a halt when he saw their handsome visitor.

Emily could sense Andy's temper start to flare, like a fire beginning to take hold. She could read what was behind those chilling eyes and was afraid of what was to come. A strange silence hung in the air, like dust; you couldn't see it, but you knew it was there. Feeling awkward, Emily gabbled, 'This is Donovan, our new neighbour. He's just dropped in to say hello.' Emily felt her body begin to shake;

she folded her arms over her chest to try and steady the tremors. She had a huge lump in her throat and felt lost for words. *Oh fuck, I'm in big trouble now.*

'Right then. Well, you better come in,' snapped Andy, pointing towards the kitchen. Emily noticed Andy's body puff up, like in a predatory stance. His muscles seemed to tighten and flex; he resembled a silverback gorilla. No chest-beating, though knowing Andy as she did, she assumed that would soon follow—a show of masculine strength and superiority. Emily followed the two men into the kitchen, her head bowed, lost in a place of torment and confusion. *Please don't mention that we've spoken already . . . What if he does? How will Andy react?* She kept her fingers crossed on both hands, hoping it would bring her luck. Her inner voice mocked her; luck was something that hadn't been on her side for years.

Emily focused when she heard Andy's order: 'Grab some glasses.' She knew from his tone that it wasn't a request. It was typical that alcohol was the first thing on Andy's mind. Emily considered rolling her eyes but thought better of it; she wasn't that brave. She searched the kitchen cupboards for glasses, overwrought and fretting about the outcome of this little get-together. She couldn't tell how it would play out with Donovan here.

Andy gave a stern cough, which she took as an instruction to get a move on. Donovan was already seated at the kitchen table, opposite Andy. He placed the prepacked flowers on the table in front of him. She could feel her heart beat faster with fear, like she was a baby bird in a cat's jaw. Finally, she found the wine glasses; they were at the back of the cupboard and bore a layer of fine dust, given that they'd not been used for years. She ran the glasses under the tap to give them a quick but thorough rinse, her thoughts flowing as fast as the running water. *How do you host a visitor?* Since living there, she hadn't had any. *How will Andy expect me to act? Should she pour Donovan's wine first, offer him food or snacks?* She realised her mind had wandered again when Andy gave another cough. The awkward silence was still there. She could practically taste the tension lingering in the air and turned towards Andy, seeking his approval. With a nod of his head, he snapped at her to hurry up. She scuttled to his side and with trembling hands, set down the three glasses on the table.

'I'm more of a beer man. Always thought wine was for poofs, but it'll do,' said Andy, smug at his own remark. He checked the year on the label, as though he was some expert. *What a moron.* Emily kept her thoughts to herself; he was definitely no wine connoisseur. She almost wanted to laugh at his inexperience, after seeing the supermarket brand name on the label, but fought to restrain herself. Instead, she blushed crimson red, embarrassed by his ignorance.

Andy glanced at her, his brows furrowed and mouth in a hard line. She struggled to compose herself and stop the grin that kept trying to creep into the corners of her mouth.

He poured the wine, filling each glass to the rim. 'So, settled in have you?'

Emily was shocked that Andy was engaging in casual chitchat. *Maybe I'm wrong. Maybe it will be good for both of us to have a new neighbour.* But she couldn't stop the unwanted images pecking at this notion, images of Andy throwing Donovan out by the scruff of his neck. Still, she couldn't believe that Donovan had actually made it into their home and was sitting at their kitchen table. She continued to fret.

'Just about. I didn't have many belongings to move in with,' said Donovan.

'Didn't catch the name.' Andy gulped a mouthful of wine from the glass like he swigged from his beer can.

'Donovan.'

'Donovan? What kind of bloody name is that? American? Or were your parents spaced out hippies?' Andy laughed, spraying wine from between his teeth, as though it was an inside joke only he knew the punch line to.

'Irish, actually, after my father.' Donovan held his own and brushed off Andy's statement with ease. Emily wanted to say 'good for you'. Her mouth curled at the corner and she smirked, she couldn't help it. She was glad Donovan had stood up to him.

Emily knew Andy was naturally arrogant, but, at that moment, he seemed to be enjoying the male company. Or maybe he was being a first-class prick and it was all pretence. Emily didn't say a word, she just fumbled with her glass, moving her finger around the rim. She couldn't remember the last time she'd taken a sip of red wine—any wine for that matter—it seemed like years ago. Neither could she believe that Andy was being nice, or that another guy—a handsome one at that—was sitting at her kitchen table. It was as though Andy had flipped a switch and found an ounce of humanity. Emily looked at Andy, wide eyed, waiting for his instruction; she didn't know if she was allowed to drink the wine or not. He nodded his head and she took a tiny sip. The flavour clung to her taste buds.

What can he say while Donovan's sat there? She knew she was pushing the boundaries. Andy waved his hand in the air to grab Emily's attention and patted his knee. She swallowed as much of her wine as she could in one mouthful, not knowing when she would have the chance to have more, then followed his instruction. Uneasily, she got to her feet and sat in Andy's lap. She felt embarrassed at being summoned like a dog in-front of Donovan; she knew her husband was showing off his ownership of her and demonstrating his dominance. She wondered whether Donovan had already labelled her as submissive.

She didn't want to cause a scene; that would have been disastrous. And even though she shouldn't, she liked looking at Donovan. She knew Andy was enforcing his supremacy because she hadn't sat on his knee since the beginning of their married life. She balanced awkwardly on the edge of his knees as she tried her best to keep some distance between them, but Andy pulled her closer until his stomach was pressing into her back. He then placed a firm, vice-like grip around her tiny waist. She considered that he wanted to appear like a regular loved-up couple, but there was nothing natural about it, and she sensed Donovan's unease.

'It was nice talking to you the other day, Emily. It's good to know I have friendly neighbours. Moving to a new place and getting to know new folk, well, it's a worry,' said Donovan.

OMFG! Emily couldn't believe her ears. His words rattled around her head loud and clear: *it was nice talking to you . . .* She didn't know how to respond. The room felt like it was closing in on her. *What was Andy going to say? Or <u>do</u>?* She felt a lump in the back of her throat but managed to swallow and form an awkward smile in Donovan's direction. She nodded her head in acknowledgement. Her stomach started to churn again and every hair on her body prickled. Everything was happening so fast. She felt Andy's body tense beneath her. She'd hoped he hadn't heard Donovan's words correctly, or that they hadn't registered, but it was too late for that, the damage had already been done. Emily felt pain as Andy squeezed his arm tighter around her waist and dug into her ribs. She tried not to show any discomfort and used her best poker face. She couldn't give away any clues to her discomfort, it would only bring further consequence.

'So, Donovan, you married?' Andy's tone was harsh.

'I was, but unfortunately, Helena died two years ago. I needed a fresh start. I'm trying to get my life back on track.'

'Well, fella, there are plenty of single women out there waiting for a young one like you.'

Emily knew what Andy was getting at, as he placed emphasis on the words 'single women'. *He's so inconsiderate, what a horrid thing to say.* Emily quickly added, 'Sorry for your loss.' For a moment Donovan's eyes locked on Emily's as he felt the sincerity of her words. He responded with a gracious smile.

Andy firmly tapped her on the arm and said, 'Drink up, wife.' Emily could tell that Andy disapproved of Donovan, and though she thought the comments he'd made were horrendous, she knew better than to challenge him. Her stomach felt like an industrial washing machine at high speed. She wished that this introduction could be permanently erased from Andy's mind, but there was no hope of that. Andy got to his feet abruptly, throwing Emily from his lap, causing her to stumble awkwardly before she straightened herself out. Andy had already extended his arm, and with a firm grip he squeezed Donovan's hand. 'Nice to meet you, and good luck with finding Mrs Right.' He ushered Donovan out the front door, tension pulsating from every pore, as though he was fighting an inner demon that was ready to consume the Earth itself. As he passed Emily he muttered under his breath, 'Fucking whore.'

Donovan had barely left the premises before Emily felt Andy's disapproval. His name calling was bad enough; she'd already accepted that he would take it to another level. As he walked towards her, he grabbed a fistful of her hair. He twisted it into a tight ball until his knuckles turned white. Her scalp stung. He then dragged her to the sitting room and she whimpered under his brutal touch.

'You dirty fucking whore,' he bellowed, like a monster not a man, his inner evil tangible—the husband she hated but couldn't find the strength to leave.

Emily could hardly catch her breath. 'Flirting with the neighbour, you dirty whore. I fuck you for the first time in years and you practically throw yourself at him.'

'I didn't! I'm not!' she protested, beginning to cry. She knew what was coming and tried desperately to make Andy understand. 'You don't understand . . . I was just hanging out the wash . . . '

'I understand alright!' he snarled.

Fuelled by anger Andy ran into the kitchen and, for a moment, Emily thought she was safe. But within seconds he was back with the bunch of flowers and the empty wine bottle in his hands. He didn't give her time to run for cover. He tossed the flowers on the floor and stamped on them then dropped the bottle on the floor. He lunged forward and yanked her hair for a second time. His face was mere inches from hers. *Too close.*

'I understand alright, whore.' He dragged her across the living room; it felt like her hair was being pulled from its roots.

Quaking and cowering before him, her legs felt weak and she flinched repeatedly as her body submitted to his rage. He was so close that she could feel his spit spray her face as he ranted, His breath smelled like the stale dregs at the bottom of a bottle. He was so furious he was shaking. His temper was foul, and his temples pulsated.

'So sorry for your loss . . .' he mocked.

'I was just . . . '

'Just what? I suppose you hang over the fence every day, flaunting yourself, showing off your tits, waiting for Mr Nice Guy to fuck you.'

'Don't be ridiculous.' Emily tried to take a step back, but his hand was too fast. His palm struck her face with such force that she lost her balance and landed on the floor. She squinted at him and saw with horror that Andy was lifting his leg, getting ready to strike. His boot repeatedly slammed against her back—his favourite target. The pain increased with every strike. She pleaded for him to stop, crying out with pain. 'Sorry,' she screamed, even though she had nothing to be sorry for. She managed to pull herself into a ball, her hands wrapped around her head, in a bid to protect herself. She yearned for cover.

'That's it,' he bellowed. 'I know what you want. You want me to fuck you, hard!'

'No,' she protested, knowing her pleas wouldn't make the slightest difference.

'Gagging for it. Tell me you're gagging for it!'

Emily gulped and begged him to stop. *What's the point?* All she could do was brace herself. With brute strength Andy pushed at her chest until he had her pinned to the living room floor. She couldn't break free, and there was no point struggling, it would only provoke his rage further. She stilled her body, conforming to his need, as he yanked at her panties, pushing them to the side. He brutally forced his fingers inside her.

'You want more?'

Emily didn't answer. She tried to find a place in her head that he couldn't reach, where she could blot out what was happening. But she knew she had no choice, that all she could do was submit to his vicious assault.

'Tell me how much you want me inside of you.' Again, Emily remained silent, which irritated him further. He rammed his fingers into her more forcefully and she whimpered at his rough touch. At that moment she even wished he'd put his wicked hands around her tiny throat and squeeze the life out of her. *It would be better than this.*

'You want more?' he said again. Finally, she whispered, 'Yes.' She wanted to scream at the top of her voice, but no matter what she said or did, it wouldn't make a difference. He was nothing but a cold-hearted bastard. Andy grabbed at her dress with one hand. The flimsy fabric offered no resistance as he yanked it off. Emily felt even more helpless, with only her underwear for protection.

She could see the wildness in his eyes, like a feral animal. His breathing became more exaggerated. Emily had seen his anger many times, but she'd never felt as afraid as she did in that moment. Andy appeared dehumanised, with a savage hysteria; there was no turning back for him. Emily had to comply with his demands. She remained unresponsive as he penetrated her viciously, pounding hard into her like waves crashing against a cliff. Soon enough, he pulled out.

He then replaced his cock with the stem of the wine bottle, ramming it inside her. Emily screamed in agony. 'You want Donovan? Here's his gift. Drink up!' he mocked. He grabbed the top of her arm and squeezed it so hard his fingernails broke her skin. Emily wept, tears streaming down her face, yet she remained still.

Slowly, he slid his leather belt from around his waist. Emily squeezed her eyes shut. 'Please, no!' she begged, but his temper had passed the point of no return. He raised it high above her stomach. Without an ounce of remorse as he brought the belt down with force, and whipped her stomach, once, twice, three times. Emily let out a string of high-pitched wails each time the leather made contact with her delicate skin. Andy looked right at her, into her eyes. Beads of sweat were crammed across his forehead and his grin could have melted stone. His grip on the belt slackened, as though he'd run out of steam. *Is it over?*

Emily winced when she saw that his stature told a different story, as he dropped the belt and leaned forward. He pulled back his arm and clenched his fist. She felt the full force of him as he punched her in the face. Her head ricocheted off the floor with the impact. He followed up his punch with more kicks from his boot. Emily felt sick and disorientated; the room was spinning, and she couldn't breathe. *Please let me die . . .*

Before she could even raise her head, he was on her again, his weight restricting any movement. She shut her eyes tightly and brought her hands up to shield her face. She cried like she'd never cried before. She squealed when she felt a pain like a hundred tiny needles; he'd sunk his teeth into the flesh above her left breast. Searing pain shot through her entire body and she squirmed beneath him. Quivering on the ground, covered in blood and feeling helpless and not worthy, Emily didn't move for some time. As abruptly as it started, Andy got up and left her lying on the floor.

Her bloody, battered body was a mess. She was covered head to toe in bites, scratches and bruises. She turned on her side and pulled her legs into the foetal position. As a final reminder of his brutality he struck her again with his boot before walking away.

Emily's back ached, as if every rib and limb was falling from its seam; her whole body shook from the trauma. Imprints from the soles of Andy's boots covered her entire back. She could hardly move; she'd felt pain before but never like this. It was complete and utter agony. Her hands moved to her stomach; it felt as if something inside had torn. She could feel dampness between her legs. Her first thought was that she'd wet herself. She placed her hand under her skirt and gingerly touched her brutalised swollen parts, assessing the damage. Her fingertips became covered in his semen mixed with her urine and blood.

Emily screamed. At that, Andy came back into the room and warned her to be quiet. As he turned to leave again, he put a finger to his lips. His facial features tight, he sneered, 'What would the neighbours think?' He gave a shallow laugh.

She felt lightheaded and didn't move from the spot for some time. She couldn't, even if she'd wanted to, it hurt too much. Silently, she sobbed. She could see her husband's shadow as he left the house, left her in agony on the floor. His twisted words replayed in her head. She wished she was dead. *Anything would be better than this. Death would be better than merely existing in this hell . . .*

CHAPTER 6

The next day, Andy got ready for work. He put on his uniform and boots so polished you could eat your dinner off them. It was just another day on the job, he'd told Emily . . . but that was not entirely true. He drove the usual route but passed the station; he continued for a few miles before pulling up outside a rundown house on Benson Lane. The garden fence was covered in weeds and the windows of the house were fifthly. It was Andy's place of birth, the place where he'd shared memories with his mother. Even though his childhood home held bad memories it was the only thing he still had from his youth, and he couldn't let go.

The house hadn't been maintained nor cleaned in years. The electric and gas had been cut off ages ago. It looked abandoned, yet it was fit for purpose in Andy's eyes. Emily knew nothing about the house; according to Andy, it was none of her business. As far as Emily knew, Andy had no contact with any of his family—he'd told her he was an orphan and an only child.

Andy paced the creaky floorboards. He told himself it was Emily's fault. Emily had caused his temper to flare. *Who the fuck did she think she was, flirting with the neighbours?* All he craved was Emily's submission, yet she dared disobey him by fraternising with some pretty boy. It was her fault. She'd provoked him. She'd practically asked for a firm hand. She knew which buttons to press and how she made his temper boil. He scowled at her audacity—*how dare she look at and speak to another man?* Marriage was sacred. *A woman should know her place.* He'd taught her that lesson often enough. Andy didn't need convincing; in his head he'd done the right thing, Emily needed to be taught that a wife should comply with her husband's need for control. After all, she belonged to him, so it was obvious that he could take her and do as he wished. It was her duty to attend to his every whim. *Stupid bitch.* She knew the rules, but one look at Mr Fucking Neighbour and she'd forgot her place. Andy owned her, like a possession he wouldn't part with. He couldn't comprehend why she needed to be reminded so often. As a wife, she should greet him with open arms, feed him, and open her fucking legs.

She can't even carry a child. The useless cunt can cook, but the rest is missing. She'd become weak. His mother hadn't been weak—far from it; she knew how to cater to a man's needs. Every time Andy looked at Emily whimpering before him, she repulsed him.

In a dark, damp, cold room of the house on Benson Lane, the wick of a candle flickered as it burned down in the glass bowl it had been placed in. At the window, heavy velvet curtains were drawn; the absence of light made it virtually impossible to see.

A putrid smell hovered in the air, and the temperature was close to freezing. It wasn't Tina Clayton's home, and she wasn't safe. It was far more sinister than that—this was her prison. Tina's mind painfully imagined every dark thought possible. She always arrived at the same conclusion—she was not going to get out of there alive. Her attempts to escape had always failed.

Her muffled sobs made little difference to the outcome, as Andy forced her to sit on a wooden chair in the middle of the floor. Tina's hands had been bound tightly with heavy ropes, and her feet secured to the chair's front legs. Her arms bore red friction scars and were tied to the wooden spindles of the back rest. She couldn't move a muscle, although she'd tried on many occasions. Her senses were fading, diminished by her dark surroundings, but she was more than aware of Andy's savagery.

Tina couldn't recall how long she'd been captive by the hands of the madman. She'd lost track of time and hadn't seen any form of daylight for so long. She didn't have the capability to speak either; Andy had put a stop to that. He'd used a household needle and blue thread through her once-pink lips and sewn them tightly shut. Tina recalled the pain; with every stitch, tug and pull, she'd yelled on the inside. Tears had flooded her cheeks and her whole body had trembled and twitched as he'd pushed the needle through her flesh. Her body was numb, due to the freezing temperature, and she'd soon become dehydrated from a lack of water. Her lips had looked like crazy paving and had become infected with unsightly yellow pus. Dark black circles hung underneath her eyes, and her face was gaunt and ghostly white. Her skin was pale, and her naked body was practically transparent. She was on full view, with heavy bruising everywhere. Semi-conscious, she tilted her head on hearing Andy's footsteps. *Oh, shit! He's here ...* Her heart rate amplified. *Please let me die.* She fought the fuzzy feeling with what little energy she had left. She couldn't take his punishment any longer and she squirmed against the ropes in the hope she may break free. *What's the use? I've tried that before. I'll never escape this hell . . . never escape him.*

Andy entered the dark, musty room where he had Tina captive—his private prison that had become Tina's personal hell. Annoyed by the situation with Emily, he felt the need to rid himself of his frustration. Every limb ached for release. Tina heard his boots rhythmically clip the floor as he strode towards her bound, tormented body. Aggravation oozed from his pores. The flicker of candlelight highlighted the anger on his face.

He mumbled something; she couldn't make out what it was he said, but she could tell his mood was not good.

In what he thought was an act of kindness, he wedged a plastic straw between a tiny gap in her stitches. 'Drink,' he ordered. Tina sucked at the straw, her only lifeline in the godforsaken place. The water was cold and refreshing and it soothed her dry, parched throat. She couldn't get enough of it and greedily gulped the liquid before he pulled it away from her. Andy's head told him to get rid of Tina. *I've had my fun.* He was in a shitty mood; his whore of a wife had been the cause of that. His mind exploded with ways he could administer his authority.

He looked Tina over from head to toe. He took in her nakedness and his eyes lingered over certain parts of her body. Excitement rumbled through his core; he felt a rush of adrenaline pump round his body and into his cock. He had the power to dispose of this woman before him. He could control her. He felt alive—he felt like a god. His subject would quiver before him.

Tina didn't make a sound—she couldn't. It was her fault she was here; she'd pushed him over the edge. Andy had no reason to justify his actions. Tina deserved it. She shouldn't have opened her pretty mouth. He called it justice, delivered his way.

Andy liked Tina's silence. He also liked her body. She belonged to him, and he would brutalise his possession before he discarded her. *I may even replace her with another . . .* But this was more than a question of need or ownership; Tina had made it personal. *No woman will ever make a fool out of me.* She'd made a mockery of the wrong man. *I'll never let it go.* He had something to prove. Andy hated women that talked too much. He hated the way they whined and protested. Tina had brought this on herself, the day she said too much. She'd gone one step further than the others, and Andy had to put a stop to that. Tina wouldn't speak out again.

Andy felt that women in general didn't understand that real men despised their endless gabbling bullshit. They needed to know their role in the world and he was a great teacher. He would make Tina understand her wrongs. *How I'm going to make her suffer for her actions . . .* He wouldn't crumble; his mother had said so on many occasions. He had strength and he would prove it. His mother had taught him to take what was his and what was owed to him. In Andy's head he was a dominant man, not a walk-over. He was masculine and powerful; it's what his mother had always expected of him, and he was not going to disappoint her.

Andy pulled up an old wooden chair from the other end of the room, positioning himself in-front of Tina. There were mere inches between them. He talked about his day without any interruption; he liked it that way, he liked her silence. He was the master of his sadistic needs, but to him, his actions were justified. He liked that he could fuck Tina whenever he liked, any way he wanted, without permission, and without any protest or petulant pleading. It was Andy's way of ridding the frustration that accumulated in the pit of his stomach. He turned it around with a punch and a kick, only then did he feel relief. It was gratifying. Bliss. He'd feel on top of the world, a genius. No questions asked, he'd feel untouchable. His cock strained against his trousers. He needed a release.

CHAPTER 7

Fourteen months previous, Andy had been in a bar. He'd ordered a pint. He'd noted that the head was too big, but he chose not to complain; he was more concerned with something else. A few seats away a woman wore a short skirt. Her shapely, tanned legs were a little too exposed and her bosom spilled over the cut of her blouse. She was completely unaware that Andy had followed her from a few streets away. She couldn't have known that she bore an uncanny resemblance to his mother. Andy felt the need to get close to her.

She'd fiddled with her mobile and, when she looked up, Andy had smiled at her. He'd asked the bartender, 'What's she drinking?' He sent a glass over, with his compliments. She seemed pleased by the gesture and accepted the drink, mouthing 'Thank you' over the crowd. *She would thank him later, he'd make sure of it. Nothing is for free.* Andy smiled back but was displeased that she had other intentions. He watched her every move—the way she eyed every man that glanced in her direction. *She's desperate.* But she hadn't looked at him that way, and he'd felt annoyed. She had no standards or integrity; he thought he should teach her a few lessons in respect. *She should have at least requested my company—that drink cost eight fucking pounds. Ungrateful bitch!* Andy heard her phone ring. Her ringtone was *I Gotta Feeling* by the Black-Eyed Peas. He smirked. He had a feeling alright, one that squirmed in his pants. The phone stuck to her ear, her face dropped from a smile to a state of annoyance. Andy couldn't help but eavesdrop her conversation. Her date was a no-show. *Dressed to kill with no playmate. How ironic . . .* He would receive his payment, and

45

soon. He'd ordered another pint, followed by another, then a whiskey chaser. He was waiting for the right moment. He wasn't alone; in his head his mother's voice sang, 'You're no good. You're a waste of space, a failure, you're a poor excuse for a man. Bet you can't get a hard on. Bet the ladies laugh at the size of your jimmy.' Andy had thrown the whiskey shot down his throat in one gulp to drown out his mother's taunts. His subconscious replied: *I am a man. I can prove it.*

It was 9.30pm when the woman with the shapely legs had left the bar. Andy picked up his coat and followed a few steps behind. The sound of her cheap heels tapping along the pavement irked him. Her head was hung low; she was looking at her phone. Social media. She hit the 'like' button on someone else's story. She'd checked in at the bar but had no story of her own to tell. Date night had been a failure.

A few streets further and the lane turned narrow, surrounded by heavy shrubs. They had only the moonlight for company. Andy had felt a thrill; his head was crammed full of whispers and the rush was hard to contain. In his head women were all the same: they flaunted their assets and took gifts from strangers. With adrenaline pumping around his body, he'd take his prize. His eight pounds of flesh. *Money well spent.* Suddenly, he sensed that she was agitated, so he strove to be lighter on his feet. He didn't want to arouse her suspicion as they come towards a bend in the lane. Andy was only a few steps behind the woman, masking her footsteps with his own. He'd reached out and grabbed her by the hair; with the other hand he'd muffled her mouth. Paralysed by shock, the woman didn't make a sound, though fear shone out of her wide eyes.

Andy had hitched up her skirt until it rested around her waist. Eagerly, he'd pushed her pants to one side and slammed her body against a fence. He'd thrust his cock deep into her. He pumped away at her, chasing the rush.

She'd asked for it. She'd wanted it. He felt so masculine. She wasn't his first and she wouldn't be his last. He took his eight pounds' worth, and once he'd finished, he'd scuttled off into the darkness, feeling satisfied with his payment.

The lady trembled as she called 999. She could barely speak. The operator repeated their words, 'Which service do you require: police, fire, or ambulance?'

Hysteria had taken over. 'R-r-r-rape . . . I've been raped!' she'd screamed.

'What's your name?'

'Carla Walker,' sobbed the woman.

CHAPTER 8

Emily glimpsed her naked, battered body as she passed the mirror. 'You deserve it, you whore.' She heard Andy's voice as clearly as if he was there with her, but it was all in her mind. She couldn't believe the ferocity of his rage; she'd recalled every horrific detail from the previous evening—it was stamped into every nerve-ending. 'Here's Donovan's gift . . .' She felt sick as she remembered how she was violated with the bottle. *I can't take it anymore. I hate him. Why is he doing this to me?*

Emily tried to make sense of what had happened. She couldn't; she just didn't understand why he felt the need to assault and punish her. *Surely Andy knows I'd never be unfaithful?* The truth was, she felt some guilt, because the first moment she'd set eyes on Donovan she'd actually thought about it. She was too afraid, though; it would never happen, it was pure fantasy. She remembered Andy's scowling face, twisted and fierce, the look of hatred in his eyes before he'd thrown his clenched fist into her face. The impact as she'd heard her nose crack still made her teeth grind. She willed herself forward, towards the mirror, to take a closer look. The image that stared back at her was unrecognisable. Black circles surrounded her pale blue eyes, and her nose appeared to be broken; it was bent slightly to the right. *Maybe it's just the swelling . . .* There were specks of dried blood, like freckles, on her face. Her eyes fell on her stomach and she stared at the marks Andy's belt had made, the grazes on her knees from where he'd pulled her by her hair along the carpeted floor. Bites, scratches and bruises were evident, like a map of carnage. *I can't do this anymore.* Emily had to face facts, things would never change. She'd never escape this nightmare. Even though she prayed for a miracle every night, she knew in her heart that one day he'd beat her so hard she would probably die. Her muscles ached, and every bone and sinew in her body screamed with pain as she tried to move her weary limbs; even the hair follicles on her scalp stung. Her existence was on a path towards destruction, either by Andy's hands, or because her mind had shattered into fragments.

She stared at the stranger in the mirror for what felt like forever. She was ashamed of what she'd become and wondered how her life had come to this. She knew she had to get out, but how? She'd toyed with the idea on many occasions, but she had no means of escape. She wracked her brains: *where would I go, where could I hide?* The answer was soul-destroying: she had nowhere to go and no one to help. Both her parents were dead, and she hadn't a friend in the world.

Anxiously, she searched various drawers in the house, hoping to scrape up some cash—even a few coins. She had no income or money to call her own. Andy had separated her from everything. *Why have I let this happen?* She felt trapped, isolated, and her options weren't good. She couldn't ring the police, Andy was the police. She sat and rocked back and forth, like a child, her mind spiralling.

The future seemed like a dark, heavy, looming cloud. A nightmare that she couldn't wake up from. She could still smell Andy's stench on her skin; she felt sick, contaminated. She had to rid his scent from her body. She moved to the shower, her mind and body both numb. Her skin felt dirty, unclean. It stung when the water hit her battered skin. *Oh my god, it hurts so much. I can't take any more.* She huddled in the corner of the shower, the warm water cascading over her broken shape. She wished she could disappear like the water flowing down the drain. She spotted a razor and a pack of blades on the bathroom shelf. They called to her.

Maybe that's the solution? She shook her head. *What the hell am I thinking?*

A voice in her subconscious told her to run. *Run wherever your legs take you. You must get out! Take control and leave. Find the strength and run . . . run anywhere he isn't.*

I can't! She tried to ignore the voice in her head. *I don't have the energy.*

For God's sake, stop being a victim and go! The whisper continued. *You must do it right now. Next time you won't be this lucky. He'll kill you.*

She remembered something her mother used to say: 'You make your own luck.' Maybe this prompted her, perhaps it was something else, but at that moment Emily couldn't distinguish fact from fiction. She couldn't remember dressing or combing her hair, nor flinging the front door open and racing out into the street. She didn't dare look back. Her legs were moving in one direction and her mind the other, contradicting her every step.

She turned left at the corner of one building, into a car park. She was wandering like a lost sheep on a hillside. She walked down the high street and towards the unknown; she didn't know where she was going or where her feet would lead her, but she carried on. Nothing looked familiar. She hadn't been out for years and the whole world seemed alien. Her lungs heaved from her pace and sweat lay on her brow. She stood for a moment, blinking rapidly at the passing cars, dazed and confused.

A police car was coming towards her. *Oh my god, is it him?* She quickly scuttled behind a bin and stayed there for several minutes, petrified to look. When her breathing steadied, she felt safe to carry on. The street lights seemed brighter than she remembered. Her head was spinning in every direction, swirling like a merry go round. She willed her feet to move on—*anywhere but home.* She knew she had to keep moving, even though it hurt. Her head down, she fought the voices in her head. This time, they taunted her: *Don't do it! He'll find you. You have nowhere to go. He won't just hurt you for this, he'll kill you. Even if you sleep on the streets, he'll track you down . . .*

CHAPTER 9

Twelve months earlier. A Friday night, and Andy was in the Red Lion. The bar hosted a variety of clients. One room was the stereotypical bloke's pub, with its regular drinkers and Sky Sports on the widescreen TV. Visitors often frequented to sample its well-stocked bar of ales from around the globe. In the other room was a small dance floor, with a DJ banging out dance classics; this was always Andy's last stop. She'd drawn his attention the moment he entered the bar. He couldn't keep his eyes off her. She wasn't hard to miss, a red rose amongst a bunch of lilies. It was almost as if she was calling to him.

His eyes had fixated on her for the entire evening. Instantly, Andy could feel the urge, a need to be close to her. *I will have my way with you.* The corners of his mouth turned upwards and he'd licked his bottom lip. The woman wore a tight-fitting red dress; her big breasts bulged at the cut like they were trying to escape. A peculiar feeling of familiarity swam over him as he remembered red was his mother's favourite colour. The two women shared a resemblance; he couldn't fight the urge to reach out and touch her. Shuffling through the crowd, he'd ordered a drink while watching her every move, his emotions stirred, and his body aroused. The woman's date appeared twenty years her senior; he wore an expensive suit with Italian leather shoes and a gold wedding band. In comparison, the woman had looked cheap.

The music blared. After a few more drinks the woman stood on her plastic heels and moved her body seductively to the beat. Everyone stared. Andy knew her type. *Flaunting her assets for all to see. An exhibitionist, striving for a man's attention.* He recalled watching the swaying of his own mother through a crack in her bedroom doorway. He hadn't known why he'd been so intrigued with the woman, all he knew was that she'd reminded him of home.

She'd held Andy's attention, for all the wrong reasons, perhaps, but he didn't care. He had to have her. He watched, along with everyone else in the bar, as she flirted with every punter—but not him. Batting her long, fake lashes and pouting her full lips, Andy could see she was a tease. Andy had felt jealous and somewhat invisible. He'd tried think of a way to grab her attention, but he decided to bide his time. He overheard that her name was Tina. *Sums her up. Tina is a slag, with everything on show. She needs a firm hand.* Andy ordered another drink and eavesdropped on their conversation. She'd talked too much, and he noted she had a stain of red lipstick on her top teeth. *She needs taming, toning down.* Andy had been irritated from her lack of interest in him, yet he still felt strangely attracted to her.

He'd waited patiently until the bar closed, never letting her out of his sight once. Tina was all over the old guy like a rash. It was obvious now that he hadn't been her date; he was probably just some bloke she'd pulled earlier in the night. Tina clung to him, yet he didn't seem that interested in succumbing to her. *Maybe she's a hooker?* She'd displayed all the characteristics. Andy couldn't stop the feeling of annoyance that washed over him. She was his type.

She tried to kiss the old guy on the cheek. He'd brushed her off with apologies. Awkward in his stance, he'd climbed into a taxi and left her behind. Tina had watched the taxi's rear lights disappear into the distance. She looked clumsy in her heels and her face was awash with disappointment and the hours spent impressing the old guy to not even get a lift home or exchange of phone numbers. Tina had strutted down the street and shrugged off her loss, accepting that she would face another lonely night at home. Five minutes later, Tina had headed towards Rumley Street. It was dark, and the other pubs were turning out. There was a scuffle between two drunks across the road that caught Andy's attention, but he had other, more prominent things on his mind. The aroma of Tina's cheap perfume had lingered in his nostrils; Andy waited to pounce. At that point, thoughts of his mother popped back in his mind. *There's a distinct similarity but I can't put my finger on what it is.* His emotions stirred, and with Tina in his sight, and masking his every footstep with hers, Andy felt the thrill, the need, adrenaline. He was already hard. Tina was going to dance to *his* tune.

CHAPTER 10

10 months previously: in all Andy's years on the force he gave it his everything. *And how did society repay him?* A suspension, followed by a polite notice asking him to resign while the investigation went ahead. He was furious; he'd given his life to his job. He questioned his colleagues' loyalty, only to learn he was a laughing stock. *Surely the lads in the office know I'm a good cop? It's all I've ever wanted. How can my peers turn their backs on me on the account of some ten-a-penny cheap whore? Believe her over me?* Her words had wrecked his career, and how pay back was a bitch.

Every murmur or whisper he heard consumed him. He'd become the butt of the joke, mocked and ridiculed, and it ate away at him—a constant irritability he couldn't tame. Until now he'd been respected, one of the lads, but in the flip of a coin the moment had gone, and things were out of his control. The service meant everything to him, since the very first day he'd put on that uniform. He knew he was a good cop; he always produced leads and completed paperwork on time. He'd always maintained his duty within the force with honour, and he was well respected within his workplace, until that bitch Tina Clayton opened her pretty mouth. *Why could they not see, he'd only been fulfilling his duty as a man . . . Tina needed a firm hand and she'd begged him for rough sex.*

He couldn't comprehend why she'd leaked information on his private life. He knew she craved a dominant man. She had a lot to answer for the day she jeopardised his career. Andy would never forgive her, not now, not ever; she'd provoked that inner darkness that frequently loomed inside. He did what his instincts told him to: *he would make her pay.* Tina would wish that she'd kept her pretty little mouth shut, Andy would make sure of that. He couldn't shake that day from his brain. It was almost as though he constantly relived the same day. The day that Tina Clayton had ruined his career and blabbed about his private affairs to the cops. She wouldn't talk again. Andy was going to put a stop to that, permanently.

May 11th was like doomsday in his mind. One day that Andy would never forgive or forget. It was the day that bitch Tina Clayton made her accusation against him. And mud sticks. He was sick of pretending but he wasn't weak, he had an urge, a voice that willed on his ego and he wouldn't stop until he felt satisfied. He'd lost his job, his security, his dignity, and his home life had become a constant bore, but most of all he had lost all respect from his work colleagues. It was Tina's fault and she would receive his penalty. He would make her suffer. She would feel his wrath, his fury and the barbaric consequences.

He recalls being called into the sergeant's office, which could only have meant one thing. He remembered the dismissive glares from his colleagues. With his heart racing and sweat oozing from every pore Andy tried to defend himself. He wanted the sergeant to understand. 'Tina was just a fling, someone to offload to,' he protested, trying to hold his temper at bay.

'Look, Brooke, it's procedure, you know that. An allegation of assault has been made official and we need to follow protocol until the claims are fully investigated. Until then, you're suspended from duty.'

Andy had been furious. He'd slammed his fists onto the desk thinking about Tina's dirty mouth. *How dare she report him? She'd wanted it . . . asked for it.* 'You can't do this, Sarge, it was just a bit of fun. Rough sex, you know? You've got to understand, my marriage is a bit dormant, if you know what I mean.' Andy's temper had begun to simmer. He didn't realise how loud he was protesting and that the whole office was looking over at him, appalled. His cheeks turned purple and he became flustered. Before he could protest further, Collins and Tailor, two fellow officers, came to the sergeant's aid. He felt embarrassed as they took him by both arms and removed him from the office. 'Let go,' he snapped, shaking off their hold. He was furious and stomped to his desk. As he removed his belongings, he could hear whispers and sneers from his colleagues. He was escorted from the premises, walking the walk of shame. His whole career had gone, and through what? *The words of a cheap tart.*

His head felt as if it would explode. All he could think about was making the pretty, big-mouthed girl pay. His head found a resolution. Tina would never talk again. The women in his life, Tina and Emily, had sliced through his feelings like a knife through butter. Tina had ruined his career in just one sentence, and the day Emily had made him beat her had resulted in the loss of his baby. These women infuriated him. He only had to look at them and he felt like putting his hands around their tiny throats. But the truth was, all the women in his life had disappointed him.

He'd walked for hours that day in a state of shock, battling his internal rage. He thought back to his younger days, of his mother and how she was never home. When she was all she did was shout at the top of her voice, or she'd entertain her latest 'friend' in her bedroom. Andy wanted her to notice him. He scrubbed and cleaned until his fingers bled—for her, but his mother never once showed him any signs of affection. He didn't hate her, she was all he had; besides, she was part of him and he couldn't let go. He remembered the hunger, and how he would search the cupboards looking for scraps to eat; it was a daily occurrence. But most of all he remembered the sounds at night: the moans of pleasure, the screams, the violence. He'd put his fingers in his ears to dull the sounds. This new uncle, his mother's latest date, was getting all the attention whilst he dragged himself up in the shadows. Mocked by his few friends for wearing last year's clothes, he had holes in his pumps and a do-it-yourself hairstyle. He'd been sneered at and mocked for most of his life. He couldn't understand why women had no respect for themselves. *They needed to be taught a lesson.* He couldn't help himself . . . he had to let off steam, the only way he knew how. The way Uncle Harry did. He admired his discipline; Uncle Harry was a real man—how his mother danced to his tune.

CHAPTER 11

Years ago, when Andy was a child, Uncle Harry had bought him fish and chips, pizza and a jigsaw. He didn't cuddle Uncle Harry—he was a man of few words—but when he was around Andrew's belly was satisfied. He had a lot to thank him for. His mum always stayed in her bedroom with the door closed; Uncle Harry said they needed privacy, but sometimes Andrew peeped through the crack in the door, even though he knew he shouldn't. Often, he heard his mother moan, scream, wail and yell—Uncle Harry liked to play boxing with her—and Andrew would stick his fingers in his ears.

He felt jealous because she seemed to have all the fun. He assumed that his mother liked playing games because Uncle Harry came every Tuesday and Mum didn't seem to mind, but Andy wondered why he was never allowed to join in. One Tuesday, Andrew peered through a gap in the door; it was unusual for it not to be closed fully and he was curious.

Uncle Harry didn't like it. He shouted, 'Fucking peeping Tom! Get your ass here and have a closer look.' Andy said he wasn't called Tom—shuffling barefooted towards them, Uncle Harry grabbed a needle that had blue thread through its eye from his mum's pin cushion. 'If you peep again, I'm going to sew your eyelids shut.' Andy closed his eyes and said sorry. A slap at the side of his head made his eyes flick open and he saw Uncle Harry throw back his head with laughter. 'Leave him be,' said Andy's mum. Andy didn't know what Uncle Harry was laughing about, but his mum nodded her head towards the door, signalling him to go away.

Andy smiled a lot when Uncle Harry was about; he hoped he would bring more goodies to eat. It wasn't a one-off: Uncle Harry left half a sandwich, cold chips and some gum. Andy would sneak the leftovers into his room. After a while, the gifts were more like scraps and empty wrappers, so Andy just stayed in his room when Uncle Harry visited, piecing together the jigsaw he'd been given. Andy loved the jigsaw; he found concentrating on the tiny pieces blocked out the sound. *At least Mum is playing boxing. She's happy.*

Late one Tuesday, way after Andy's bedtime, Uncle Harry brought some friends over for a party. Andy had never been to a party. There was a lot of booze, salted nuts and a huge bumper pack of crisps; Andy felt a thrill eyeing up the goodies. He sat in the corner of the room, his taste buds already drooling, imagining how he could take some without being noticed. Once the party moved into his mother's bedroom, he jumped to his feet and quickly grabbed a few packets, scuttling to his bedroom where he ate greedily.

The sounds of heavy metal music echoed, and rowdy cheers bled through the thin wall to his room, even after Uncle Harry had left. Andy just turned up his radio. He wished the others would hurry up and leave, the partying was boring—no balloons or cake. Andy was exhausted; he'd had little sleep, even the socks he stuffed into his ears didn't muffle the sounds. He laid under his duvet praying for silence, just ten minutes would do. Hours later and daylight shone through the narrow gap in the curtains. Andy couldn't hold it much longer, his bladder about to burst; he needed the toilet, desperately.

He scuttled across the hall and saw through his tired eyes the last two men leave. He noticed one of them had bloody knuckles and was carrying a four pack of beer. *Maybe he fell over.* The unsightly pair didn't even glance his way as they stomped out. *Maybe I have superpowers and I'm invisible.* Even though they couldn't see him, he saw that they'd enjoyed the party, because the pair laughed a lot as they walked out the door.

They left the front door wide open. Andy waited till they were down the path before he shut it. It was freezing cold and you could see your breath in the air. The heavy metal music was still blaring from his mother's room. Andy wanted to turn it off, he needed some sleep and he knew it would be another day off school. His mother's bedroom door was ajar by a few inches, which was unusual; she liked her privacy. Andy quietly pushed the door open.

He stood in the doorway. He'd never seen his mum totally naked before and his eyes lingered on her buttocks. She was sprawled, face down, on the bed. Her hair covered her face. She usually wore a dressing gown and her hair in a messy bun on the top of her head. She looked a mess. Andy didn't know what to do; the situation was strange, and it didn't feel right. He called her. 'Mum! Mum!' She didn't reply. *She must be asleep, maybe she'll be mad if I wake her. She must be cold, too.*

Andy rubbed his tired eyes, he wanted to sleep. He walked over to his mother's stereo, his back pressed against the wall, and turned off the screaming racket. The constant thump was giving him a headache and his ears rang with a funny hum as he slowly tiptoed back out. His belly rumbled and alerted him to the familiar pang of hunger pains. Andy was glad that the blokes had left the nuts and crisps—it would satisfy him for now. The booze was gone, but it didn't really interest him anyway.

Andy munched his way through half the stash and hid the rest in a drawer in his room; he didn't know when he'd next eat. His thoughts told him this wasn't the norm, that his mum was sick, but he was exhausted and couldn't help yawning. He washed his face in cold water before returning to his mother's side. 'Are you okay, Mum?' he asked, whilst wiping his tired eyes. She was still face down but managed to mumble a reply; he couldn't really make out what she said. Andy nudged closer; she looked hurt and he spotted bloodstains on the grey bed sheet. Andy didn't like the sight of blood, it made him feel queasy. *What do I do?* He rubbed his head, he'd never seen that much blood, and there was a lot.

He prodded her bare skin. She felt cold and didn't respond. *Maybe I should roll her over, put some plasters on her wounds . . .* Andy struggled as he tried to move his mother's battered frame. Eventually, he managed to roll her onto her back. She whimpered at the movement. Her eyes were swollen and there was a huge gash on the side of her lip that was still pouring with blood. She had cuts and bruises along the length of her body.

'Did Uncle Harry win the boxing match?' Andy asked curiously. She gave her head a gentle nod in acknowledgement and pointed to the dresser. Andy assumed she meant the pin cushion, not the mobile phone or the cigarette packet. He picked up the needle that was already threaded with blue cotton through the eye and forced it through his mother's bloody lip. *Open wounds need to be stitched . . .* He remembered watching a programme about hospitals; he liked playing doctor, he would make it stop and fix his mum. He recalled stitching an old pair of socks, it was easy.

He stitched and stitched until the blood had ceased and his mother had passed out. Andy felt good, he'd stopped the blood from seeping. *Mum will be proud of me. Surely, she will appreciate my efforts . . . maybe she'll buy me pizza!* He stood for some time, smiling, proud of his handywork and dreaming of his reward. Picking up the grey bloodstained bed sheets, he covered her up to her waist to keep her warm. He felt a need to stay longer, watching over her. His eyes hovered over her exposed breasts. He was intrigued and watched her bosom heave whilst she breathed deeply in her sleep. After a while he crawled back to his bed. That morning marked the first time Andy touched himself; it felt soothing but stimulating. He'd accomplished something, which had stirred the excitement in him. It felt good, natural, to hold himself in his hand. As he threw back his head in orgasm, he felt euphoric. The boy was no more.

CHAPTER 12

That evening Andy arrived home at the usual time. All he could think about was dinner. He was starving, and he hated that feeling—it infuriated him. But today was different, the routine had faltered. The usual aroma of a cooked roast didn't meet him when he walked through the front door. When he entered the kitchen there was no dinner on the table or joint in the oven. Furthermore, there was no wife. *Where the hell is she?* He could feel the frustration building inside him, like a dog growling whilst baring its teeth. He searched the house, overwrought. He knew this was not normal practice for Emily. *What the fuck is she playing at?* Andy knew something was wrong and he'd already begun to plot her punishment. *Maybe she's hiding? Surely not.* He couldn't make sense of it and stood for some time in confusion. He tried to think where she might be, but his hunger made it hard for him to concentrate. He glanced at the kitchen table a second time; his dinner was absent, but his temper was present. He noticed the door still had the key in the lock and that the television was switched off. Andy was beside himself, engulfed in rage. 'When I find you, you're in for it!' he bellowed. Furious, he ran through the house again, throwing open every door and checking every room before taking the stairs two at a time.

In their bedroom, he noticed that the bed hadn't been made and there were damp towels in a heap on the floor. The shower was still running, too. His emotions began to get the better of him; he clenched his fist and punched the wall several times, splitting the plaster. He then picked up a dressing table chair, tossing it across the room, before sweeping his arm across the dresser, hurling toiletries in the air. Like a typhoon he lashed out at anything that stood in his way, leaving scenes of destruction behind. It was obvious Emily had gone.

How the hell could she just vanish? Andy couldn't comprehend it. All he felt was anger, a tidal wave of rage; he felt as if he could take out an entire village. 'Emily! Emily!' he spat through gritted teeth. His mind tried to focus. *Maybe I'm wrong, maybe she's in the yard . . . So why the fuck is the housework not done? And where the hell is my fucking dinner? She wouldn't have dared go out, would she? No fucking way!*

He moved to the back door. *It's the only place she can be.* Irritably, he called out her name. The back yard was empty. He struck out at the plant pots with his foot, which spilled over. He stood, sweating, thinking of recent events, when an unwanted thought snuck in. *I bet she's with that neighbour, Donovan!* He gave a feral growl. Images of Donovan fucking his wife swam before his eyes, Emily moaning in pleasure clouded his thoughts. He felt as if steam could come from his ears, he was at absolute boiling point. *That's it, she's having an affair. It's the only place she could be. The fucking whore must be with him. I'll show her!* He thought about Emily flaunting herself over the fence, pegging out the washing, showing off her tits . . . gagging for it. His rage fuelled his footsteps; without hesitation, Andy sprinted to the neighbours like a husband possessed.

Donovan's car was parked in the driveway. Andy didn't hesitate. He burst through the front door in a mist of fury, not once considering knocking or waiting to be invited in. 'Emily? I know you're here!' he yelled.

'What's going on?' Donovan appeared from the kitchen.

'Where the fuck is my wife?' Andy glared at Donovan, his brow furrowed with fury, his whole body screaming and pulsating with aggression.

'What the hell are you talking about? Emily isn't here!' Donovan looked confused. 'I think you need to leave.'

Andy ignored him. He ran upstairs, two at time, bellowing Emily's name and a mouthful of obscenities. 'Emily, you stupid whore! Get down here.'

Donovan had seen and heard enough. He put his coffee down and ran after him. 'What the hell is going on?'

'She's here, I know she is! She's screwing you.'

'Calm down, Andy, she isn't here. You're talking utter nonsense.'

'Calm down? I'll show you fucking calm!' Before Donovan could duck, Andy threw a string of punches towards him. Donovan was no stranger to violence; he'd been confronted many a time whilst carrying out surveillance. Being a detective paid the bills, but it also had its downfalls.

Over the years he'd encountered a lot of Andys, as well as scraps and punches. In his line of work, he came across the dregs of society—so many that he couldn't formulate a figure. To get results he'd worked alongside, and even partied with, some of the most ruthless people you could imagine. Donovan had resigned himself to the fact that there was always a cost when following a lead.

'Get the hell out!' yelled Donovan. He pushed Andy with force, roughly guiding him down the staircase. They scuffled on the stairs before Donovan got the better of Andy, giving him one final push out the front door.

Picking up the phone, Donovan sighed. He called his colleague and long-time mate at the station. 'Cooper, give me everything you have on my neighbours, Andrew and Emily Brooke—from way back, no matter how insignificant.'

'Leave it with me, I'll see what I can do,' replied Cooper.

Donovan ended the call and sat down, shaken by the unwarranted intrusion. He thought of Emily, the way she quaked in her husband's presence. He'd witnessed it with his own two eyes. He felt sorry for her and blamed himself and his introduction; he knew he'd probably messed everything up. *What the hell had just happened? How do I get myself into these situations?* Donovan had looked into the eyes of a madman and understood fully why Emily seemed so subdued—why she was so haunted and lost. Yet he'd allowed his own scheme to override any thought for her.

One thing was for sure, her husband was a wife beater and a bully. Donovan had witnessed the signs before on others. Donovan thought of his own wife, Helena; he felt sadness daily, and there was no running away from it either. How he wished he could hold her in his arms again. With Helena's image invading his thoughts, he snivelled into a soggy hanky, then scrunched it into a ball. *Christ, give yourself a shake. This could be the lead that you've been waiting for.*

Donovan jumped in his car and crawled the streets for hours, searching for Emily. He felt some guilt, as though he had provoked her misfortune. His eyes widened as he scanned the dimly lit streets. He drove cautiously along the kerb at a steady speed, the window wipers beating frantically as they battled heavy downpour. *What's the use? She could be anywhere. Maybe Andy's already found her and she's home?* Donovan spun the wheels and the vehicle turned around. As he did so he caught sight of a lone woman sitting on a bench; she appeared to be using the branches of an old oak tree as some form of shelter. *Is it her?* He squinted as his eyes adjusted to the darkness. *It is her! It's Emily.* He felt relief then his thoughts turned to worry. He didn't have a plan. This wasn't on the cards. *Now what do I do?*

He noticed that she had no coat and sodden slippers. Her hair was soaking wet and it hung limply around her pale face. She was shivering from the ferocity of the rain. Slowly, he pulled up at the side of the road and wound down the window. 'Emily! Emily . . .' he called, but she didn't respond, instead staring vacantly into space, lost in her own thoughts. He'd seen enough terrible scenarios to know she was in a state of shock. 'Emily, its Donovan. Let's get you out of the cold. You must be freezing.'

Emily could hear him, but his voice was clouded by the conversation running through her mind. Eventually, his calm voice broke through and it finally registered that she wasn't dreaming. *Donovan?* She looked at him with glassy eyes, her teeth chattering. Her body trembled. She felt like she'd been hit by an electric storm—she felt frazzled and wiped out.

Donovan got out of the car to stand beside her. He took off his jacket and wrapped it around her shoulders. Emily flinched at his touch.

'You're safe,' he whispered.

Emily looked up at him. Like a lost soul, her face held no expression. *What do I do? How did this happen? Where do I go? I have no one. I have nothing, I am nothing. I may as well be dead.* Taking her by the hand Donovan guided Emily to her feet. She gave in to his gentle tug, but her feet wouldn't move, it was as though the signals in her brain had malfunctioned. Donovan stayed calm and gently coaxed her forward, towards the passenger door of his car. Her hands felt icy cold and her lips had a blue tinge. Everything about her screamed pure and utter shock. By the look of her battered face, there was little wonder why. 'I can't go home, I just can't,' she pleaded. 'I've no money and nowhere to go.'

'Look, we'll worry about that later. Just get into the car.' Donovan's voice was soft and gentle.

He managed to get her into the passenger seat. Emily felt Donovan pull the seat belt across. As he strapped her in, the pain in her body took hold.

Donovan noticed the bruising to her face. It was clear she'd been badly beaten; he hoped for her sake there was no internal damage. 'You need the hospital,' he said, concerned.

'I don't want to go to hospital. That's the first place he'll look.' As she begged Donovan not to take her home, she noticed a scuff mark above his right eye. 'What happened to your face?'

'Your husband,' he replied.

Emily burst into tears. 'I'm sorry,' she whispered.

'You have nothing to be sorry for.'

CHAPTER 13

July 21st the previous year. Andy had been stalking Tina Clayton for weeks. *This one's different. Maybe she's the reason I've kept up this game for so long?* He couldn't shake the fact she bore an uncanny resemblance to his mother. All he knew was that he was in the midst of an unhealthy obsession.

The red dress was like a second skin to Tina's curvaceous body; it was an outfit that tormented his memory. Red was his mother's favourite colour. He was drawn to Tina—the way she walked with a swing in her hips, much like his mother had whenever Uncle Harry was around. Tina also oozed desperation like the scent of a cheap perfume–much like his mother, who always had a date on her arm. Andy knew Tina was seeking a mate. He would take her as his playmate, and she would dance to his tune. He fantasised about her constantly, he imagined how she would feel and how she would squirm. He decided to bide his time. He'd step in during her moment of need. He'd spend some time with this one. She required more of his attention, more than any of the others. That moment couldn't come soon enough.

Andy stood in the shadows, a predator waiting to pounce. He recalled the other woman, Sarah. He called her a 'weekender'. That was the amount of time she lasted. He also thought of the others: the alleyway whores, Carla Walker—his quick fix—but none of them fulfilled his need the way Tina did. He liked to revisit memories in his mind, he summoned them often. He thought Sarah was the opposite of his mother, yet there had still been some similarities that drew his interest. Maybe it was the fact her bosom bulged and spilled from a blouse two sizes too small, or perhaps it was the auburn hair that hung over her face?

But Sarah hadn't complied. He'd bound her, stitched those full lips together—and *still* she'd murmured and moaned. Tina was different. He would keep this one, he just knew it. Tina was a keeper.

Tina Clayton had met Andy Brooke in a bar. She was thrilled that he had a good job as a police officer. Over the years Tina had dated too many jobless deadbeats, so she welcomed Andy's interest. He seemed quite a catch. Often, Andy would shower her with expensive gifts. She loved the attention. The relationship flourished from the very start. It consisted of wild, rough sex, and being wined and dined. Tina finally felt like the rest of her loved-up friends. She was tired of signing up to dating apps, having to going out on the pull, searching for Mr Right.

It wasn't long before Tina glimpsed Andy's temper. He turned persuasive and brutal. But she didn't want to be an old spinster, so she became submissive. Andy had a way of persuading her that was hard to resist. Whether it was the diamond earrings, the designer watch, the fancy meals out, or loneliness, Tina craved a man more than her freedom. She'd felt lonely for some time and feared being left on the shelf as her buddies all settled down. Tina was done with sitting in bars, looking desperate; doing so had played havoc with her purse and her confidence. She'd been stood up and let down on many an occasion. She had no luck with men, but Andy had stayed, and that was all she wanted in a man.

A few weeks into their relationship and Tina was getting ready for their usual Friday night date. Time had passed quickly for them, and it felt like a whirlwind romance. That was the evening everything changed. Tina didn't stand a chance.

There was a knock at the door. Tina has just got out of the shower; she glanced at the clock and presumed Andy had arrived a little early. She ruffled the towel through her hair and applied mascara and lipstick. The knocking came again, more impatiently this time. Tina slipped on her silk dressing gown. 'One second!' she called, checking herself in the mirror.

She opened the door as she pulled her dressing gown tighter to hide her damp body. 'Oh, Tim. I wasn't expecting to see you.'

'Sorry, you left your paperwork on your desk. I knew you had a deadline, and I was passing, so I thought I'd save you a trip and drop it off.'

Tim handed over some notes. 'Thanks! You're an angel,' she said. 'I owe you one.' She winked at him playfully.

'A Krispy Krème doughnut with my coffee first thing Monday would be a good start,' Tim laughed. 'Enjoy your weekend.' He gave her a quick wave as he began to walk down the path.

Andy turned the corner into Tina's street. He was singing along to the radio, dressed smartly, ready to take Tina to a restaurant. He suddenly yanked at the handbrake. The car came to a sudden halt. He took in the guy who was strutting down Tina's drive, smiling and waving. Andy could feel his temper rising; hot, like explosive lava. *Who the fuck's this guy?* He sat in the car for a minute, watching her face. He noticed how it glowed and how brilliant her smile was towards some guy walking away from her door. *The bitch!* Andy's eyes locked on Tina's silk dressing gown. He mumbled under his breath, 'What the fuck is she playing at?'

Andy gripped the steering wheel like he was squeezing the neck of a chicken. His temper continued to simmer as he watched the guy get into his car. His mind flooded with obscenities. *Fucking whore! Lying cunt! I'll fucking show you.* He saw Tina give a final wave to her colleague.

Tina suddenly noticed Andy sitting in his car. *Why isn't he getting out?* She looked at him, confused, waving at him to get out of the car. She was unaware of his disapproval.

Andy's subconscious sneered. *You should have known better—women are all the same. One man in, another man out.* It was obvious Tina was screwing the guy . . . having an affair. *Tina belonged to him, did she not understand that? I'll make her understand.* He wasn't going to share her.

His head hurt. He thought about his mother. He wanted to lock himself in a room and put his fingers in his ears, but his temper fuelled his actions.

Each time Andy struck Tina she begged for him to listen. 'Tim's just a work colleague, that's all!' But Andy knew women only spoke lies.

'You'll tell me next that he's your uncle,' mocked Andy.

'What are you talking about, my uncle?' she yelled back at him.

Andy's fists and boots did not cease until Tina's body bore his stamp in shades of black and blue. Tina sobbed. She'd never suffered like this. 'Get out!' she screamed. She quaked in fear but wouldn't submit so easily. She needed him to understand he'd crossed a line.

Her neighbours overheard the commotion and called the police. Later that evening the event was put down to 'domestic disturbance'. Tina didn't want to press charges; at that moment in time she didn't need the hassle, and she couldn't really afford time off work. She'd already concluded that it was over between them the minute he'd raised a hand to her.

The next day Tina's phone rang repeatedly. She refused to take Andy's calls, and after a while she blocked his number. Andy felt his insides squeezing. *Who the fuck does she think she is, treating me this way? She's cost me a damn fortune, bloody wining and dining and fancy gifts.* He expected a return. He hated the fact she'd played him for a fool. He needed to see her, he needed to take what was rightfully his, and he wouldn't let it rest. No woman was going to belittle him. Throughout the whole weekend he'd tried to catch a glimpse of her, without success. *Maybe she needs time to calm down.*

On Monday morning, first thing, he called her at work. Tina immediately recognised the caller ID; she gave a deep sigh. *Just sod off and take the hint!* To her annoyance, he left several messages, but she still didn't answer or return his calls. Andy had no other option than to seek her out. He was desperate to be near her, to feel her.

He hovered outside her workplace for several days at closing time. To his displeasure, he couldn't catch her on her own, but he wasn't prepared to let it drop. She owed him. He watched her from a distance, laughing with her colleagues; he wondered if she was talking about him. *Was she saying he had a tiny cock? Was she mocking him?* He'd wipe that smug smile off her face. He heard his mother's words: *You're not a man. You're weak, a good for nothing freak.* He tried to banish any thoughts of his mother from his head, but her voice echoed and cackled like heavy rain on a tin roof.

He glared as he watched Tina throw back her head with laughter. Her facial expressions became distorted; as they changed, he could see his mother. The hallucination was all too real. Confused, Andy gave his head a shake, in a bid to rid himself of her mocking whispers. But his mother wouldn't leave. Her words were always there, taunting him.

Tina drove down the dual carriageway not far from her home. Andy was a couple of vehicles behind her. *How should I take her? She* will *submit to my needs.* After ten minutes she pulled into her drive. She was greeted by an elderly neighbour who was putting some rubbish in their trash bin. 'I haven't seen you for some time, dear,' Andy heard the old woman say.

'I've had a lot on at work,' Tina replied.

Margaret Smith was known as the local gazette; she could talk the hind legs off a donkey without coming up for breath. Tina had no choice but to stop and share idle chit-chat. Margaret could pull information out of anyone, even passing strangers. What she didn't know wasn't worth listening to.

Andy parked down the street and turned the engine off. He could feel his patience wearing thin as he watched Tina chat away to her nosey neighbour. *She's probably the interfering cow who phoned the police.* He'd bide his time. His whole body trembled as adrenaline pumped, his desire to subdue her and teach her a lesson overwhelming.

Mrs Smith was still rambling on when Tina caught sight of Andy out of the corner of her eye. Her heart raced. *What the hell does he want? This is getting fucking ridiculous, bloody weirdo. Why won't he take the hint?* 'I'm really sorry, Mrs Smith, but I have to pack. I'm going away for a few days and I'm in a hurry,' she flustered. Tina made her excuses and almost ran into the house, locking the door behind her. She leant against it, her head flooded with agitation. *Why won't he leave me alone? My god, now he's following me home. I want rid of him for good, out of my life forever.* Tina paced the floor, planning her next move, where to go; she needed to get away for a few days, sort her head out. *A hotel, maybe? He'd just follow me there. My mother's? Yes, that's it. I'll pack and head to Mum's.* One thing she knew for certain was that she felt uneasy. She wasn't confident enough to stay on her own with her ex stalking her. She felt unsafe. She recalled the wrath of Andy's temper and how he'd been hounding her for days on the phone. A cold shiver ran down her spine. *Why me?!* Tina picked up her mobile with trembling hands and texted her boss: *Hi, Clara, sorry for the short notice and inconvenience but I need a few days off. Regards, Tina.*

Tina shuffled towards the window and peered through a narrow gap in the curtains in the hope Andy wouldn't see her. Her eyes scanned the street for any sign of him or his car. She let out an exaggerated sigh of relief; it seemed as if Andy had taken the hint and vanished. She still felt unsettled; she knew deep down, that he wouldn't stop. He wasn't likely to take the hint easily. She had to face facts: Andy had already beaten her, harassed her, called her at work then followed her home. For the first time in Tina's life she felt afraid. *I need to get out of here, and fast.* She'd feel safer at her parents' house, they'd know how to advise her. It would do her good, she hadn't seen them in months.

She called her mother but there was no answer. She didn't want to leave a message and have her worrying, deciding instead to try her again later. As she ended the call her house phone rang. Tina ran to it, thinking her mother was returning her call, but the display showed Andy's mobile number.

That's the final straw, I've got to put a stop to this. She wasn't going to be a prisoner in her home because of some lunatic. Tina called the police and requested advice on how to obtain a harassment order. She also came clean about the previous assault, so they had a true picture of events. The operator took her details and gave her a log number, saying an officer would contact her in due course.

Andy drove around the city for some time, trying to formulate a plan. He didn't want to raise suspicion or allow Tina's nosey neighbours to catch a glimpse of him. The voices in his head wouldn't still; they mocked and taunted him. *She played you for a fool! She's laughing at you! She thinks you're a weak man—not even a man, a failure!* Andy wiped the sweat away that lathered his brow. He told the voices to disappear through gritted teeth. But they wouldn't leave, which only made him more furious.

By 9.20pm that evening Andy had returned to Tina's street, parking up a few feet away from her home. He turned off the engine and waited for an opportunity. He still had a key tucked away in his wallet. Even though he was alone, he couldn't stop the constant nagging in his head. The voices fuelled his illusions; they spewed laughter and mockery. *Do it now! She's a whore, a dirty good for nothing cheat. Teach that bitch a lesson . . . she's made a cunt out of you. You're pathetic and weak; a boy, not a man.* He closed his eyes for a moment, willing the voices to stop. *Wait till the lights are off and she's sleeping. Slip in through the back door, like a black cat against the night . . .*

Half-an-hour later Tina went to step out of her front door. Andy saw that she was carrying a travel bag in her left hand and seemed to be in a hurry. He'd used the darkness as a cloak, hovering behind a bush for a signal that the right moment was upon him—that she was tucked up in bed. Now that she was leaving the house his whole body stiffened and his temper soared; his plans would have to change. *Where the fuck was she going? Fucking whore, she must be going to stay with her latest fancy man.* Before he had chance to think clearly, he was upon her. He knocked her back into the hallway and closed the door with the heel of his foot. Tina was petrified and instantly dropped the bag. She tried sprinting away from him—her aim, to run through the living room to the back door—but he was too fast for her. He knocked her to the ground and took what he believed to be rightfully his. *Tina was his.* He brutalised her, hard, on the carpeted floor, punishing her with every thrust, whilst simultaneously slapping her. Her sobs were muffled by the hand he held over her mouth. Her pleas seeped through his fingers and tears escaped from her wide eyes.

Moments later, Andy reached climax. He climbed off her and pulled up his zip, before walking away without a word. Tina remained on the floor. Tears stained her face and her clothing was ripped at the seams; it looked like a wild animal had clawed and shredded the material. Neither spoke; the only sound was Tina sobbing.

After a few minutes had passed, she began to think it was all over and that Andy had left. She glared up at the ceiling. Her temples throbbed. *How could he do this to me?* She felt as though her whole world had caved in. It was hard for her to accept that he'd raped her with such savagery. Her body felt sore.

She didn't recognise Andy anymore, but then again, had she really known him at all? He'd pulled the wool over her eyes. *How could I have been so blind? A wolf in sheep's clothing . . .* She blamed herself. *It's your own fault.* She'd been so desperate to have a companion that she'd settled for the first guy she'd met. How he'd deceived her. Every inch of her body ached. Her face was bright red from his unrelenting slaps. She felt shame from being violated by the man she'd once loved.

Andy sat in the dark corner of Tina's living room, silently, in her armchair. A voice whispered in his head: *Silence her.* He watched her scuffle around on her hands and knees as she searched for her mobile phone. Her attempt at rescue failed when he leapt from the chair.

Tina screamed and desperately scrambled across the carpet. Andy's stocky stature easily overpowered her small frame. He snatched the phone from her grasp and threw it to the ground. He glared at her as he stamped on the unit repeatedly, until it was in pieces. Tina quaked in his presence. She feared for her life. *Who is this monster?* Andy leant over her; he was so close that she could feel his breath on her face. 'Help!' she screamed. *Maybe the neighbour will hear me and call for help.* Andy grabbed her cheeks and squeezed them between his fingers, forcing her lips still. He then moved his other hand to her tiny throat. 'One squeeze and I may not stop,' he mocked, applying more pressure. Tina felt faint as his hands squeezed tighter. She didn't see it coming, it happened too fast. Andy thrust his head forward. It connected with hers with such force that she was knocked out cold.

CHAPTER 14

The wind and rain never ceased; the day was downright dreary. Emily could have easily passed for a castaway that had just been rescued from a desert island after suffering for months. She gave the appearance of some wildling that had been released into the modern world. her trauma was ever-present.

'You'll be fine,' Donovan reassured her.

He cupped his arm around Emily's waist as he guided her up the steps to safety—away from her monster of a husband and out of the horrendous weather. A room on the second floor was free at the Anchorage Hotel; it wasn't the Ritz, but it was warm and comfy, and it was the least he could do in the situation. Emily was a mess, a battered and bruised mess, and she needed not only shelter but also some rest. Donovan had tried to talk her into going to the hospital, but she'd protested in floods of tears. He knew he couldn't take her home—Andy was his neighbour, after all, and a violent one at that. This was the only solution he could think of at short notice.

He sighed to himself. *What have I got myself into?*

The hotel room was basic, but it had all the essentials. *Anything's better than the streets.* Emily glanced around; a wooden table and two odd chairs sat in-front of the window. There was a small sofa and a double bed. Immediately, she felt panic. Donovan noticed her concerns. 'It was the only room available,' he said.

'You don't have to do this,' she whispered.

'Look, let's just get you rested and warm.'

Emily needed time to think. The truth was, she couldn't think straight at all. Everything seemed a blur, except the pain—that was real. She didn't know how to thank Donovan for the roof over her head, but she also worried about tomorrow and the next day. How would she survive? The outside world seemed so big and daunting. She realised that she'd let one man take control of every aspect of her life. She owned nothing but the clothes on her back.

Emily let out a shiver—a mixture of coldness and anxiety. Her skin was mottled blue, and her wet clothes clung to her body, showing her skinny frame. Dirty, soggy slippers adorned her feet and her hair was so wet and limp she could easily have passed for a woman possessed—a character from a horror movie. But this nightmare wasn't fictional, it was Emily's reality. No matter how hard she tried to push Andy from her mind, his brutal face clouded every thought.

'Why don't you get a warm shower and some sleep? Things will seem a lot clearer tomorrow,' Donovan suggested. He felt that he was hovering; he didn't know what else to say or do for the best. All he could think about was making Andy pay.

Emily nodded her head, an automatic reaction to any request made towards her. It seemed a good idea, her body shivered and jerked; she was frozen to the bone. She shuffled towards the bathroom.

Turning on the shower, the small room suddenly filled with steam, which mirrored Emily's clouded mind. She hung her dripping clothes on the radiator. The spray from the showerhead hit her body and stung, which brought back painful recollections of the blows from Andy's fists. She sat under the spray for some time, as if her mind and body were thawing from the reality of her escape. *What have I done?* She blamed herself. *I shouldn't have left. I'm so scared, what do I do next?* A soft tap on the door still managed to startle her and her body stiffened. She had no idea how long she'd been lost in her thoughts, though she was aware that the warmth from the water was the only comfort she had at that moment.

'Everything okay in there?' asked Donovan, concerned.

'I won't be long.' Emily wondered if she could face Donovan again. She felt terrible and looked worse than she felt.

Slowly, Emily pulled on the tatty, thin hotel dressing-gown that had been hung on a makeshift peg on the back of the door. It was well-worn and off-white in colour. *Oh, what does it matter? It's warmer than my wet clothes.* She wiped away the steam from the mirror. A crack ran down the centre. She related to this; she, too, was broken. Her face was swollen and bruised, and her eyes were bloodshot. Her wan skin and deep frown lines made her look much older than her years. *I certainly don't wear stress very well.* She smoothed damp hair from her face and tried to plaster on a smile, but it was no use—she had nothing to smile about.

She was grateful to Donovan, and thankful for his interference. *Shit, Donovan! What does he think of me, looking like this? What shall I tell him?* It all felt too much; she wasn't sure how to communicate her feelings, or how much she should tell him. She gripped the sink as if it was a lifeline for several minutes. She breathed heavily and felt overwhelmed by her emotions. Her head told her to open the door. *You can't hide in the bathroom forever!* She exhaled and straightened her shoulders. *You can do this, Emily.* She'd become a good actress, moulded by her husband's hand. She could pretend everything was okay—she'd had years of training. Her fingers rested on the handle as she hesitated.

She eventually opened the door. Donovan was sat on the floral couch. He stood as she neared, but she instantly shied away from him without making eye contact.

'How are you feeling?' he asked.

'Fine,' she lied, still averting her eyes. She felt embarrassed, not just because of how she looked, but also the circumstances they were in.

'Get some rest. It looks like you've been through the mill. I'll come back tomorrow and bring you some clean clothes then we can plan what to do next.'

Emily didn't move. Her feet wouldn't budge; she hadn't been left to her own devices or without instruction for years. Thoughts rushed her mind. *What if he doesn't come back? What if Andy finds me? What happens next?* She'd always followed Andy's lead, his 'list' still imprinted in her mind. She quaked at the thought of being alone; everything seemed like a giant hurdle. She found her voice. 'Please can you stay with me? I really don't want to be on my own.'

Donovan knew she was desperate, a woman on the edge of despair and defeat. He felt sorry for her. *How come I always get into situations like this?* At times he felt like the Pied Piper. Still, he reasoned, she was in a state, and even though he didn't need to, he felt responsible. That he'd had a stake in her misery.

'Alright. I'll take the couch, you have the bed.'

For the first time in years Emily slept the whole night through without waking. Maybe she was simply exhausted from the mental and physical trauma, or perhaps it was because she felt safe—for now.

Emily opened her eyes around 8am. Immediately, thoughts of Andy jumped into her head. She couldn't shake him; his words rang in her ears. She sat up and ran her fingers through her hair, then caught sight of her rescuer.

Donovan was awake. His hair was ruffled, and his suit was crumpled; he'd slept fully-clothed on the couch. She felt guilty until she caught sight of Donovan's warm smile.

She smiled back. 'Hi.'

'How are you?' he asked.

'Feeling foolish and sore.'

'Want to tell me about it?'

Emily shook her head. She wasn't ready yet. She hadn't come to terms with it herself.

'I'm going to find you some breakfast,' he said. 'Won't be long.'

Donovan headed towards the door as Emily said, 'I'm really sorry for dragging you into this mess. I didn't think he'd hit you.'

'Don't you worry about me. It's just a scuff, I'm as tough as old boots.' Donovan smiled again, giving her a small wave before he left.

Emily felt horrified that Andy had struck Donovan. Then again, he'd beaten her back and blue for years, so why it was a shock, she didn't know. She tried to move without jarring her aching limbs, but it was impossible. She gritted her teeth with every step as she headed for the bathroom. She'd become accustomed to pretending she felt okay and had put a brave face on things while Donovan was around.

In the bathroom Emily stared in the mirror. Her reflection revealed a pale, gaunt face; she hardly recognised the person staring back at her, she was practically a stranger. Her blue eyes sat atop dark, puffy circles. A gash on the top of her forehead had started to scab. Her shoulder-length hair hung in a shaggy mess, which only seemed to highlight her battered features. *What must Donovan think of me? A weak woman with a madman for a husband.* The bruises on her body were more obvious than the day before. She wore the shame, like a coat for all to see. Andy's image hovered in her mind, of when he was stood over her, raining down blows and offloading his temper. She knew she would never be rid of him. He was in her head, under her skin, like a form of bacterial contamination no antibiotic could kill. She'd walked on eggshells for so long, submitting to his requests, that she'd lost herself—given up on the fight. She tried to remember a time when their marriage was good, but there was no happy memory to recall, just sadness; he'd drained every bit of strength from her, until she was broken and damaged beyond repair. She'd been blinded by his control and could see no escape from the wreck she'd become.

She remembered the first beating he'd given her. It was when she was seven weeks pregnant, and he had the gall to blame her for the loss of their child. Although Emily would never forgive him, she knew damn well she couldn't have raised a kid in that environment—it was lucky that it never existed.

Forty minutes later and there was a knock at the door. Emily panicked; she froze, listening only to the thrum of her heartbeat. She considered escaping, but her options were limited, unless she wanted to throw herself out the second-floor window. *What if Andy has found me? What if it's him?* She paced anxiously, biting at her fingernails until they were sore. *What if Andy hears me and my footsteps?* She sat on the end of the bed gingerly, holding her breath, not daring to make a single sound. Her heart raced, and every muscle stilled, as though paralysed by fear. Startled by another knock—louder this time—she retracted her limbs whilst keeping her eyes fixated on the door.

She heard Donovan's voice and exhaled. 'Emily, are you decent?' he called.

She let out another sigh of relief. 'Yes.'

Emily hesitantly opened the door, just in case there was a nasty surprise waiting for her. Donovan smiled as he walked in. He carried two shopping bags and a tray of Costa coffees. The aroma of bacon wafted through the air and Donovan passed a sandwich over. Emily was ravenous. Her stomach grumbled loudly, much to her horror; she hadn't eaten that day nor the previous one.

'How you doing?' asked Donovan.

'Okay, considering.' She shrugged her shoulders, wincing with pain. She didn't really know how she felt at all.

Donovan parked himself on the couch next to her and took a bite of his sandwich. 'You've had a lucky escape,' he said, through a mouthful. 'Don't be upset with me, but I reported the incident and made an appointment for you at the station. You can't let him get away with this.'

'No, I can't! You don't understand.' Emily immediately felt anxious. She couldn't go and talk about her private affairs at the station. *What on Earth was Donovan thinking?* Emily felt her eyes fill with tears.

'Please don't cry,' he soothed. 'I've seen enough to know that Andy needs to be stopped.' Donovan licked some brown sauce from the corner of his mouth.

'But . . . you don't understand. He works at the station. His workmates won't entertain what I have to say. They won't believe me, and Andy will go mental.'

Emily began to sob. Her head swam with images of every attack she'd encountered by his cruel hand. She couldn't go to the station; she wasn't prepared to face it, or reality. Not yet.

'It's the right thing to do. Just because he's a cop doesn't mean he's above the law.'

'Donovan, you don't know him like I do.' Emily's voice shook.

'I know his sort, that's good enough for me. And I've seen the bruises.'

'I don't feel strong enough. What am I supposed to say? What if Andy's at the station?'

'Look, don't worry about that. I'll be with you every step of the way,' Donovan reassured her.

Emily couldn't get her head around why Donovan was being so nice. *Surely, he has better things to do than babysit me?* It was the first time anyone had shown her kindness and she didn't know how to reciprocate. She looked him over, trying to ascertain his agenda. *What the hell is wrong with me? He's only being nice. I've just forgotten what that feels like, that's all.* She finished her sandwich and took one of the shopping bags into the bathroom. She put on the sweater, leggings and shoes he'd bought her. She was amazed that the outfit fit. *It looks a damn sight better than the hotel room dressing gown.* She thought he had nice taste and she appreciated his efforts. She just didn't know how to thank him.

'I . . . I haven't got the money to pay you back for the clothes—or the room. Andy always saw to the accounts.'

'You really don't need to worry. Let's just focus on getting you sorted.'

CHAPTER 15

Andy hadn't slept a wink. He'd drunk heavily for most of the night and hostility started to take over every rational thought. He was on a path of destruction and couldn't rein in his temper. He felt as though he'd lost the plot. He lashed out, trashing the household furniture. It was as if the Incredible Hulk had possessed his body.

He lifted the chair and tossed it across the room, followed by ornaments—and anything else he could get his hands on. Frantically, he searched every shelf, drawer and cupboard, looking for some clue as to Emily's whereabouts. *I will find you, Emily.* He reached for some comfort and grabbed a bottle of whiskey in his hand. Displeased that there were only a few mouthfuls left swishing around the bottom, he took a final swig before throwing the bottle at the wall. It smashed into tiny pieces and the dregs dribbled down the wall.

His mind was working overtime. He was infuriated by the whole situation. *Where could she be? How can she disappear without a trace? It's impossible.* His mind told him that Emily was selfish, that she didn't appreciate everything he'd given her over the years. *The ungrateful bitch . . . and still she's run away without a word.* Andy knew one thing for sure: Emily wouldn't get far. She had no access to their bank account and therefore no money at all. Neither did she have friends or family. *Where would a penniless woman go?* Then it hit him; like a light bulb turning on, he arrived at a conclusion. *A refuge. It's the only place she can be.* He pulled out his mobile phone from his trouser pocket and googled refuges in the area. The results showed two; both were just a few miles away.

Within the hour Andy was heading down to Margret Street Refuge. The harsh gales almost knocked the breath from his chest, but his anger had far more fury than the wind. As he walked, he considered ways to handle the refuge, but he already knew from his policing experience that he wouldn't get any information simply by asking. He didn't have a badge anymore and he wasn't in his uniform; with Emily missing, he hadn't felt the need to keep up the charade. He was a regular citizen, and there was no chance of him obtaining confidential information on the residents. *Bummer.* He didn't have a hope. All he could do was sit, watch, and wait patiently.

The sky turned dark, like his mood, and rain bounced off the pavement. Nothing would stop him from finding her; the thought consumed him. Settling on a bench adjacent to Margret Street Refuge his determination kept him there for hours. He pulled his hood up around his ears, his sadistic thoughts his only company. He didn't even feel the wrath of the storm or the cold. He watched the comings and goings with a keen eye, scanning every woman that came through the refuge's doors. They were hidden under a raincoat, umbrella or hood, and each time his nerve endings twitched with anticipation. But there was no sign of Emily. *Not yet, anyway.* He reassured himself that his patience would eventually be worth it, and he smiled inwardly at the thoughts of what he was going to do when he caught her. His assumption that he'd catch Emily in the act gave him a rush of excitement. He imagined her face as she submitted to his needs.

Eventually, his patience began to wear thin. Tense and furious, he paced up and down the pavement. The urge to find her just grew stronger.

CHAPTER 16

The rain bounced off the pavement and formed huge puddles in the street. Donovan held an umbrella above Emily's head and linked his arm with hers. His support and guidance were the only things keeping Emily standing. Her nerves were already shot, and her stomach churned with anxiety. *How did I let him talk me into this?* As they drew closer to the entrance of May Lane Police Station, Emily felt like running the other way. *I can't do this, I just can't.* Her head swirled, and palpitations brought beads of sweat to her brow. Her head felt light, as though she'd been pumped with helium and was floating far away. She stops in her tracks and looked at Donovan. 'What if I see him? I can't face him.' Her words were saturated by panic; she could feel her heart rate getting faster and faster. The wind seemed to be whipping past her ears. *I can't concentrate . . .* Everything in her mind seemed a blur, as though she was having a bad dream.

'I've got you,' Donovan whispered. He placed an arm around her waist and gently guided her to the information desk. Emily was unable to give her name; the words just wouldn't form. She thanked God that Donovan was by her side. She knew, in her heart and her head, that she wouldn't be able to do this without him.

Donovan spoke to the officer behind the glass. Then a voice came from far away. The second time she heard her name, it broke her dreamlike state. 'Mrs Emily Brooke? I'm Sergeant Cooper. This way please.'

'Now?' She looked at Donovan. *I don't feel ready for this.* He gave her a reassuring smile, but she needed more.

'It will all be over soon,' he soothed.

Emily felt as though she didn't have the strength to get off the chair, never mind walk. 'Go on. I'll wait here,' said Donovan.

'Come with me, please,' repeated Cooper. She gripped Donovan's hand so tightly he thought she'd never let go. Donovan stood, and together they followed the sergeant down the corridor into a side room. Emily sat on one of the four chairs gathered around a desk. She remained silent and stared at the bare white walls. She felt as though she couldn't breathe, like the room was closing in on her.

Sergeant Cooper waited a few minutes before speaking. Eventually, he cleared his throat. 'Donovan informs me that your husband has beaten you. Is that right?'

Emily nodded her head. She could feel herself trembling. The room began to spin.

Donovan gently put his hand on her shoulder. Only then did she feel some ease. 'You're safe,' he said. 'It's fine. Sergeant Cooper's here to help. That's what the police do—help.'

'You don't understand,' she whispered. 'Andy works for the police. You won't believe me, no one will. Andy knows the law.' She sobbed into her hands.

'Andrew Brooke hasn't been part of the force for nearly two years. He was suspended after an allegation was made against him.'

Emily brought her head up quickly, shocked by his statement. 'What do you mean, suspended? Are you telling me he's not been working here for *two years?!*'

'That's correct.'

'No, you must be mistaken!'

'Emily, it's the truth,' said the sergeant.

'Where the hell has he been going then, if not to work? And what allegation was made? I don't understand.' This was way more than she could comprehend.

'I can't tell you about your husband's movements, or about the allegation; it's confidential. What I can tell you is that this isn't the first time someone has reported him for assault.'

Emily's mouth went dry. 'Who reported him for assault?'

'I'm not at liberty to share that information.' The sergeant refused to say any more on the subject.

'He wore his uniform every day. He said he was under a lot of pressure from work, and that was why he lost his temper with me.' Emily choked back another sob. 'I've been an idiot. Where the hell has he been going, and who the hell has he assaulted?'

None of it made any sense. Emily couldn't believe what she'd heard, no matter how hard she tried. After several hours of questioning, Emily finally made a statement as Donovan urged her on. 'You've done the right thing,' he reassured her.

Donovan had been a rock; she couldn't have done it alone. But she still couldn't fathom what Andy had been up to, or even where he'd been going all this time.

After the interview Emily was asked to back up her allegations. Sergeant Cooper said they needed photographic evidence, too. Emily felt ashamed; being scrutinised by a camera lens was hard to take. It had been a long day full of tears and revelations; she still couldn't shake her husband's secret life from her mind. *I've been so naive and stupid.* The evening dragged, and everything seemed surreal.

It was 10.03pm by the time a female officer escorted Emily to another room for her photographs. A nurse was also present, and the photographer was female. Emily could feel her cheeks flush with embarrassment. Shame prevented her from looking at either woman in the eye. She envied their simple lives.

'Emily, can you get undressed then sit here, please?' The nurse pointed to a chair. 'We'll be with you in a minute.' It was all so textbook, and Emily felt like a number, not a human being with feelings. She felt humiliated, as though they were judging her with every glance. *Why me? Why?! I hate Andy for this.* She began to cry again, and the nurse passed her a tissue. Emily blew her nose. 'Just relax,' said the nurse. Emily hadn't relaxed in so long she'd forgotten how to. 'It won't take long.'

Behind a curtain Emily fumbled with her clothing. The tremors in her hands made it difficult. She took a few deep breaths, in a bid to reassure herself that everything was fine. She questioned why she was there, being stripped and degraded. *All because of a man. How have things come to this? I'm a wreck . . . I'm weak. A laughing stock. Damaged goods.*

'Are you ready?' called the nurse. Emily peered through the curtain. The nurse made a note in her paperwork. 'Emily, I know this is traumatic, but we're here to help. We can take it as slow as you want, but we need these photos as evidence.'

Emily nodded. 'I understand,' she said, blowing her nose again. Though she'd already undressed she couldn't help stalling. Her dignity was tarnished. She took a deep breath and stepped forward, her body on display for all to see.

The nurse prompted her to stand in-front of a white board. Her legs felt weak, her mind in a place beyond reach, but she'd surprised herself that she'd come this far. Her pale skin displayed heavy bruising; as she exposed every inch of her battered skin, Emily had to endure the indignity of baring everything for all to see. She couldn't have stopped the tears even if she'd wanted to. She didn't feel confident to look the professionals in the eye; her dignity had been stripped away, stolen from her. All she heard were the clicks from the camera as she turned this way and that, as instructed—until she was exhausted, both emotionally and physically.

CHAPTER 17

By the time Emily got back to the hotel she felt as though she'd revisited every horrific memory of her married life. Her mind seemed flooded with misery. Donovan had made a quick stop on the way back to grab them both a takeaway. As she'd waited in the car, Emily had glared through the window. It was like looking into a dark abyss. Even though the food smelled delicious, she'd never tried Indian food before. Regardless, she wasn't in the frame of mind to eat anything.

The security of the hotel room's four walls gave her some comfort. Donovan ate his food from the carton, in a hurry; he told her he had some work to attend to and needed to go. It had been one hell of a day and, even though Emily was desperate for the company, she knew Donovan couldn't be her bodyguard twenty-four-seven. He had a life of his own. Emily was just thankful he'd stood by her, in her hour of need, but she also felt guilty of the burden she'd put on him. *How can I ever repay his kindness?* She couldn't, and as she considered her next step, she realised she had a lot to learn. How to be alone somewhere other than her marital home; she told herself that Donovan leaving was good practice for the future.

'See you later,' said Donovan as he left. He'd only been gone a few minutes and she instantly felt lost. She realised she hadn't even asked him where he was going; then again, it was none of her business. As she stripped for the second time that day the tears started and wouldn't cease. *Why me? How did I end up like this?* She collapsed onto the double bed and stared at a cobweb in the far corner of the ceiling. If she'd been at home, she would have removed it instantly;

instead, she just glared as it, as though that tiny cobweb was a show of defiance. She huddled under the blankets with the TV set on. She turned the volume up louder; she needed a distraction from her thoughts. After battling with her inner self for a long while she finally gave into her exhaustion.

Emily woke just after five a.m. It was Friday morning. In the darkness of the unfamiliar hotel room, she shivered at the shadows lurking in the corners. The TV standby light flickered red, and Emily fumbled with the nightlight on the dresser at the side of the bed. She was covered in sweat as a result of her nightmares. Maybe her eyes were playing tricks on her, but for one short moment where her heart almost stopped, she thought Andy was in the room with her.

She strained to hear a noise, fully alert. She thought she could hear his voice; it sounded so close and she struggled to distinguish fact from fiction. Emily jumped to her feet. She put her ear to the door, believing Andy was standing behind it. Her head swam, and she held her breath so as not to make a single sound. *You're hearing things. It's just a dream.* She faced facts, no one and nothing was there but her imagination. She crawled back into bed but left the bedside lamp on.

Three hours later she woke again. She opened the curtains and watched birds flying free in the bluey-grey sky. She wished she had their freedom. The sun was shining, and she felt its rays give her hope. She opened the window and took in a lungful of air. *Maybe one day I will be free . . . rid of him for good.* She stood for nearly an hour—watching parents escort their little ones to school, the hustle and bustle of commuters on their way to work. It made her realise how much she'd missed out on as a prisoner in her own home. She'd been the inmate and Andy had been the warden—except in her prison there'd been no privileges, not one. She placed her hand to her stomach, remembering that once she'd held a flicker of life in there. She also remembered how Andy had put an end to that, by kicking her until she'd bled. All she'd ever wanted was a simple life, the things that other people took for granted: a family and a husband who loved her. She questioned whether it was attainable, doubting it very much. Andy had messed her up good and proper. She felt worthless; she'd forever be known as the battered wife, the weak woman, the one who had no strength. *How can I move on from this? How? And where do I go?*

CHAPTER 18

Donovan was no stranger to the case of Tina Clayton; she'd been missing for quite a while now. Tina had left no forwarding address nor resigned from her work—the only reference was a message saying she required a few days' leave. Her neighbour, a Mrs Smith, had also confirmed that Tina had mentioned packing and going away, but hadn't stated where she was going or who with. Mrs Smith had also said Tina's car was still sat in her driveway.

Tina had just disappeared without a trace, into thin air. Tina's parents were family friends of Donovan, from way back, and he'd given them his promise that he would try to find new evidence that the local police had missed.

Donovan had planned from the outset to get close to his suspect, Andrew Brooke. He'd been aware that Andy no longer worked for the police, and that he'd been previously interviewed as a suspect in relation to Tina Clayton's disappearance. There'd been a lack of substantial evidence, and they couldn't hold him. Even though Tina had logged a complaint against him, it was just hearsay. The police had established that there had been a sexual relationship between Andrew Brooke and Tina Clayton. They'd found fragments of a mobile phone in Tina's home, which was put down to a domestic incident.

Donovan, when renting the property next door to Andrew Brooke, hadn't intended on becoming so involved with Emily Brooke. He'd certainly not planned to take her under his wing. To be honest, he should have left things well alone. *But how could I have done that?* He wasn't the sort of person to sit back and let a vulnerable woman be beaten just because he'd introduced himself—*what type of man would that make me?* He felt as though he owed her, that it was his fault—that his interference had brought on her assault, but, in his heart, he'd known in that very first moment he'd met Andy that he was a bully and Emily was a victim. Donovan thought hard about the scenario. *Victims need a friend; a shoulder to lean on, someone to trust . . . and I need as much information as possible for my case, so maybe it's a good outcome for both parties.* He focused on what his gut was telling him: that Tina Clayton must have suffered at Andy's hand. He had the temper and was a viable connection, that had already been established.

Donovan feared Tina was probably dead. And like a dog with a bone, he was no quitter; he'd find out what happened. In Donovan's mind, the original alpha male, Andy Brooke, needed teaching a lesson. Donovan had to be smart and stay focused; he needed hardcore evidence for Tina's family, so they could put their daughter to rest. He pondered how Emily would react if she knew of his job and how he'd been watching them, but decided it wasn't the right time to tell her. She was a wreck and she wouldn't be able to handle the truth—not yet, anyway. He decided to remain quiet about things and see how things panned out.

Donovan thought of the day he'd met Emily over the fence. His first impression of her was that she was a dithering wreck—a peculiar woman. He'd felt no attraction to her, yet the more time he spent with her, the more his feelings were changing. He wasn't sure what those feelings were; it wasn't love, he knew that. *Maybe need. This is all wrong . . .* He battled with his thoughts. He expected that Emily would feel used if she knew the truth about his case, and that it could possibly destroy her. He didn't want to be accountable for that. He decided that, right now, Emily needed a friend, someone to trust, who could help put her on the right path. Only when her mind was strong enough would he tell her of the case. They could help each other. Emily could be the answer to his prayers, the solution to his situation. Time would tell.

CHAPTER 19

Donovan and Cooper had been friends for more than fifteen years, ever since their first day at the academy. They'd gelled like long-lost brothers. Even though they worked together, every couple of months they'd hang out together, as they shared the same interests. They did all the things mates did together: laughed, pranked each other, shared their troubles. They were both competitive when it came to a round of golf or a game of football, but it never stopped them enjoying their time together. Cooper was top of the list for best man when it came to Donovan's wedding—and tasked with sorting the stag do. The latter was certainly something to remember, Donovan smiled to himself; it would have put the film *The Hangover* to shame. What happens in York stays in York; no matter what the circumstances, they had each other's back.

Cooper was beside Donovan as he'd taken Helena as his wife. Cooper had thought of Helena as the sister he'd never had, and she'd accepted that the boys were inseparable. Cooper had been the one who'd brought Donovan home from the hospital on that devastating evening when Helena had passed away; seeing her hooked up to every tube in City Hospital traumatised them both. He was Donovan's best friend, and nothing could break their bond.

Donovan recalled the day he'd almost walked away from his job and his position as detective. He didn't, as the title demanded responsibility, and he had plenty of that. He had to forget that feeling that he'd let Helena down and concentrate on keeping his shit together. But the truth was Donovan was still angry; he harboured a grudge. He'd never brought that drink driver to justice. He'd had to accept that things didn't always go to plan. Once his grief had lessened he'd taken a new attitude and a new role, but this didn't stop him seeking his own retribution.

Donovan had been watching his wife's killer for weeks. One day, he'd watched her park up and pull out a transparent carrier bag that contained a tin of beans, a loaf and six cans of Special Brew. *So, she's not quit the booze. Has she not caused enough suffering?* He thumped the steering wheel, angered by what he'd witnessed. With every footstep she swayed in her cheap plastic heels. Her hair hung limply, and red lipstick highlighted the cigarette wedged between her lips. *How is this justice? What has she learned? Rehab, my arse.*

Donovan felt hatred rise inside him, but he had no idea at that point just how strong his anger and bitterness was, or what they would make him do.

CHAPTER 20

Cooper handed over the case file of the investigation and the interviews with Andrew Brooke. Donovan felt from the very start that he was the missing link and, by God, he was going to prove it. He just knew Andy had been the last person to see Tina Clayton alive.

Brooke had claimed Tina had been seeing another lover at the time she'd disappeared, which meant he had motive; all Donovan had to do was drag up the evidence and nail the bastard, one way or another.

Donovan mulled over the information he had on Andrew Brooke, along with the domestic disturbance complaint from Tina Clayton's neighbours, and the request from Tina for a harassment order. Scrutinising the case files, Donovan was curious about Brooke's earlier years. He took to the database, in search of anything unusual. He noted that social services had been involved with Andy's family on numerous occasions: issues around neglect, malnutrition and several occasions of truancy from school—the usual, concerning a single mother that worked the streets. During Andy's late teens there was nothing from which to draw a conclusion; it was as though he'd slipped off the radar.

Then later, like a tarnished coin dipped in cola, Andrew Brooke's record of achievement shone. He'd gained good grades and a high school diploma. He'd gone to college and, at twenty-one, passed the competitive written exams to gain a place on the Force. His academy training seemed straightforward; Andy had been one of the lads, although he had a reputation for being arrogant, which was a comment from most of his peers. At twenty-seven he'd married. He'd no known children, and his mother, Lilly Brooke, aged sixty-nine years, resided at 44 Benson Lane.

Donovan knew Andy hadn't had the best start in life and he also knew that, by having a relationship with Tina Clayton, he was now an adulterer. Then there was the call log from Tina's neighbours, about a disturbance. The officer in attendance had confirmed that Tina Clayton had been assaulted but he'd noted that she didn't want to press charges. Then came a second log, which showed that Tina had rung for advice about unwanted calls she'd received from Andy Brooke; the log recorded that she'd wanted to press charges for the previous assault.

Andy had been suspended from duty as the investigation began. The final log transcribed Andy's interview as he'd been questioned about Tina Clayton's disappearance. Eventually, no concluding evidence was found to support the investigation. Donovan knew Andy Brooke was a rat.

CHAPTER 21

When Emily first walked into the station as a battered wife, her mind had already been scrambled. Then hearing that her husband had been having an affair was soul destroying. She'd been totally unaware, and she felt betrayed but learning that this woman had been declared missing after she'd made an allegation of assault against Andy was something else. In her head, Emily already knew the answer: Andy was capable of everything he was suspected of, and she knew she'd got off lightly.

Why had Andy put on that uniform every day when he'd lost his job? It was utter madness. In her mind she ran through their last few years together, tried to retrace his steps. Their lives had run like clockwork—always to his beat, his excuses; he'd blamed his workload for his temper. For a moment she doubted what she'd been told. She felt totally confused.

Things finally started to piece together: Emily hadn't been allowed to open any mail. She assumed now that the red letters had been outstanding debts, due to the fact Andy had been jobless. What a double life her husband had led, and how naïve she had been. Andy hadn't had sex with Emily since the miscarriage years ago; that is, until recently. In Emily's mind, that wasn't sex, it was rape. Emily had never once considered that Andy had a girlfriend on the side. *No doubt his girlfriend had fulfilled his needs, then, when she'd disappeared off the radar, he'd become frustrated.* Emily was told not to call Andy at work or on his mobile. If only she'd had some clue, maybe seeing him for what he truly was might have made her leave sooner. But she'd been too scared, too downtrodden, and felt that she'd had no other option than to follow his lead.

An officer at the station had handed her some leaflets: one was for a woman's refuge, and another was aimed at supporting victims of crime. Emily's eyes blurred when she focused on the leaflets' bold lettering. *VICTIM* . . . *How has my life come to this? When did I wither and die?*

Donovan insisted that Emily stay at the hotel until she was properly back on her feet. This seemed an unattainable goal; all she felt was worthless. She hardly knew Donovan— it didn't seem right—*but what other options do I have?* She couldn't see past the end of her nose at that moment, never mind what the future held. One thing was for sure, Emily knew little about the outside world. She'd already concluded that she couldn't survive by herself, she didn't know how to.

She searched in her coat pocket and pulled out a pamphlet. 'I have the details for the women's refuge,' she said to Donovan. 'I'm sure they'll help me. I can't have you paying out for me.'

'You will not go to the refuge! My god, have you seen those places? I'm sure one day you can return the favour. I'm doing it because I want to, not because I have to. I want to help.'

'I really do appreciate your kindness,' she replied coyly.

Everything seemed easier when Donovan was by her side. His kindness and his gentle soul were both refreshing. For the first time in a long time Emily felt alive. Safe.

After weeks of care, love and attention, Emily's bruises had finally disappeared, but she knew her mind would be scarred forever. During this time Emily had grown fond of Donovan. He'd been the perfect gent, and she felt secure with him beside her. Emily had begun to gain confidence and take care of her appearance. She could talk about the weather, watch TV, take a stroll in the park; she felt Donovan had given her a glimmer of hope—a new life, a second chance to get things right. The more time she spent with him the stronger she felt. She was beginning to heal. The weeks had flown, and she felt as though she was floating above the clouds. She liked this new feeling that had replaced her fear. Very soon, Donovan had become everything to her.

Emily was dependant on him. He didn't complain; in fact, he seemed to like it. It was almost as if Donovan needed her as much as she needed him. *Could this be a new beginning for both of us . . . ?*

CHAPTER 22

December, and the evening air was cool. A breeze gently whisked away the last of the autumn leaves. Emily felt like she'd also been swept off her feet with excitement; she'd never been to the theatre before. She wore a new blue dress and cream shoes, which Donovan had kindly supplied. *He's so considerate.* Emily felt and looked like a movie star as she caught sight of her reflection in the glass window. Donovan stood at her side and she felt a flutter in the pit of her stomach. He'd offered to take her to see the Phantom of the Opera, and she was overcome. Emily's emotions were etched on her face and she had a grin as wide as the Cheshire Cat's. Her eyes glistened like bright stars in the sky. Together, they sat in the balcony, waiting for the show to commence.

Once it began Emily was awestruck by every sound and detail. She found the story heart-breaking but brilliant. Seeing the phantom, the man behind the mask, also made her think of how her identity had been hidden behind her bully of a husband; she related to the character in certain ways. She smiled or sobbed throughout the performance. She'd never seen anything as magnificent or evocative. Donovan passed her a tissue from his inside jacket pocket. He was always prepared, which she loved about him. At the end of the performance everyone stood to cheer and clap. In that moment, Emily realised she could feel something other than pain.

Scuttling through the crowds after the show, Emily loved the feeling of being sandwiched between people. She'd been isolated for so long. These were the little things folk took for granted. The streets were busy, the atmosphere full of laughter and chit-chat. They walked arm in arm through the busy crowds, looking every inch a happy couple. Emily drew in a breath; she couldn't believe how quickly Donovan had crept into her affections. She wondered whether he felt the same.

Donovan interrupted her train of thought. 'It's so nice to have your company tonight. It's nice to have a friend.'

Emily felt disappointment. She looked at his face. He wore his usual warm smile, but it wasn't really the statement she'd hoped for. *It's not a date. Donovan's a friend, he said as much already. He wants to help and that's all.* Emily was happy, regardless, and felt glad that Andy couldn't take the feeling away from her. *So what if Donovan wants to just be friends? That's good enough for me.*

As they walked back to the hotel they chatted about trivial things: the weather, their school days and their likes and dislikes. The evening had gone quickly—too quickly for Emily's liking—but she was grateful. Grateful for everything Donovan had done for her. She knew it couldn't, and wouldn't, last forever. She needed to get her act together, get a job, support herself, and stand on her own two feet. He'd told her not to worry about it, that he'd help her and that she should focus on getting herself right first. Baby steps, he'd insisted. She liked that about him— he wasn't pushy or dominant, he was the total opposite.

They stood at the doorway to Emily's hotel room. Emily felt like a nervous schoolgirl on her first date. Again, she reminded herself that it wasn't a date; it was just friendship. She wasn't good at reading situations. Was it love, lust, need, friendship? Something unusual was stirring inside her, a feeling that had lay dormant for years. She gave herself a shake. For the first time in her life she was assertive. She wanted Donovan to conform. 'Coffee?' she asked, while fumbling with the key.

'Do you think that's a good idea?' He winked playfully.

'Ha-ha, what must you think of me?' She laughed her wicked thoughts away. She was still on a high from the performance. It had been so good to laugh and feel things; now, she needed to get a grip on her emotions. 'Thank you for the best evening ever,' she said, meaning it. She grinned from ear to ear.

Before either of them knew what was happening, Donovan had grabbed her arms and pulled her closer to him. As their bodies touched, she felt a quiver of happiness run over every inch of her skin. He looked into her eyes. She paused for a moment then took an exaggerated breath and bit her bottom lip. Her arms seemed to have a mind of their own; she threw them around his neck. Donovan didn't let another moment pass, he leant into her and kissed her passionately. She responded eagerly.

Donovan had tried not to crumble or give in to his needs, but over the weeks he'd grown to like Emily a lot. When he wasn't with her, he couldn't get her out of his head, and he just couldn't resist her when she was around him. Yet, in the back of his mind, he felt guilt, which weighed heavy. He'd not yet told her the truth and the secret remained within him. He dismissed these thoughts; he could only deal with one problem at a time. Andy was the reason he'd rented the property next door. *How will Emily react to that?* It ate away at him, but he hadn't found the right time to tell her. He didn't want her to be hurt any further. She'd been through enough and he couldn't risk her running away either. He reminded himself that he was a gentleman, but something also told him he was a liar—that he was deluding her as well as himself. With that, he did what he thought was best. He prised his lips from hers and held her at arm's length. 'Sleep tight,' he said, before turning on his heel and walking away, battling his demons.

CHAPTER 23

Andy couldn't sleep that night, nor through the ones preceding it. He'd already staked out one refuge without results and his patience was beginning to wear thin. He walked through the town daily, asking passers-by if they'd seen his wife, Emily, willing his rumbling temper away. He'd hold up a photo of her to anyone that would listen. Concerned citizens had taken a glance, but no one had any information of her whereabouts. Andy persisted; he fabricated a story: Emily had suffered a mental breakdown and had wandered off. He showed concern and sadness, an act that could have won awards. He even shed a few fake tears, as he said all he wanted was to hold his dear wife in his arms once again.

He had to find her. His need to control her was more powerful than any emotion. His rage rattled under the surface; he was so mad, he felt he could quite easily snap. He felt an urge to put his hands around someone's throat as he waited outside the other women's refuge. He sat on a bench with a newspaper and watched the front door intently, waiting for a glimpse of Emily. He didn't care how long it took to find her—eventually, he would. How she would cower before him.

His eyes lingered on a figure coming out of the refuge. She looked familiar. *Could it be Emily?* Andy's stomach fluttered with excitement.

Catharine Clarke was of the same height and build as Emily Brooke, and her hair was a similar shade of auburn. She wore a long coat with the hood up; it masked her face, and as she left the refuge, she didn't realise she was being watched. It was only her second outing with no chaperone and she still felt some unease, but she knew she had to face the world on her own sometime if she was to rebuild her life. She walked nervously, with her hands in her pockets, window shopping as she made her way to the library.

Andy was a few steps behind her . . . he still thought it was Emily. His temper raged like a volcano ready to explode. *How could Emily even think of leaving me? How dare she make a mockery of me! She must pay for her disobedience, one way or another. I'll show her.* He mimicked Catharine's every move until she cut through a ginnel on Turpan Road. His pace picked up and he felt an adrenaline rush. He was almost euphoric that he'd found Emily and plans for her punishment gave him such a thrill. She would quake before him, regardless of her pleas

After some time, Catharine felt a shiver run down her spine. She was aware that someone was behind her. She didn't like it, though she wondered if this was just her paranoia. She approached a bend; there was no one else in the alley, except the person whose heavy footsteps sounded like they were gaining on her. She felt uncomfortable, but she didn't have the courage to look over her shoulder. She began to have palpitations and broke out into a sweat. *Maybe it's my imagination . . .* She tried to shrug it off; she'd made it this far and broken away from a violent home. *Things are on the up.* However much Catharine tried to reassure herself, deep down she knew something wasn't right. Every hair on her body was rigid. She tried to pick up her pace and focused on reaching safety inside the library. Before she had chance to run, she felt someone grab the hood of her coat. Her legs turned to jelly as a hand muffled her screams. It all happened so fast.

Andy pinned Catharine to the wall. Despite realising it wasn't Emily, his inner demon took things to another level. He couldn't help himself. The resemblance was too much—images of his mother and Emily swam around his head, taunting him. He pushed Catharine's face to the wall. Holding her in position, he slipped down his zip. Eagerly, he pulled out his already-hard penis, forcing himself between Catharine's legs from behind. He lifted her skirt over her hips and pushed her pants to one side, before thrusting his fingers into her. Grabbing his cock in one hand, he forced it into her before pounding and thrusting relentlessly, still with his other hand over her mouth.

Catharine was petrified, frozen to the spot like a rabbit caught in headlights. Tears stained her face and all the colour drained from her face. 'Fucking whore, you love it,' he spat into her ear. Within minutes he'd reached his peak, climaxing deep inside her. After zipping himself up he punched Catharine in her back. She slid to her knees. Adrenaline still pumping through his veins, he couldn't resist swinging his leg back. The impact of his boot caused her to hit the ground with a thud. She lay on the dirty concrete, too scared to move a muscle. Andy simply walked away.

CHAPTER 24

Two weeks later and Andy continued to search every inch of the city. He looked in every cafe and bar; his feet ached but he couldn't rest until he had claimed Emily and brought her home, where she belonged. He tried a cafe on Lonsdale Road; he'd had no joy at any of the others and this was the eleventh on his list. It was a dump of a place, a greasy spoon; however, the food looked almost edible and his stomach had started to grumble. He hadn't eaten a decent meal since Emily had disappeared. Memories of acute hunger from his childhood resurfaced and he took a seat by the window where he had a good view of the city. He fidgeted with the menu until an old woman shuffled towards him from behind the counter. *She looks as ancient as the décor.*

'What can I get you?' she asked, peering at him through her thick glasses.

'Coffee and a bacon sandwich,' Andy replied. While he had her attention, he pulled out Emily's photo and launched into his sob story.

The old woman not only believed him, she seemed eager to help. 'Oh, yes, I have seen her, with a gentleman friend. I think she's staying in the Anchorage Hotel, though I can't be sure.'

Andy didn't even give the old girl time to get back to the counter before he leapt up and ran out the door. He could feel bile rise up into his mouth as he imagined Emily with another man. *Who the fuck is this guy? He must be pimping her out—that's all she worth. She has no money, so how the hell can she afford a hotel?* Then a thought hit him. *Maybe it's Donovan . . . he's the only other guy she knows.* Andy hadn't seen Donovan around for some time. *The fucking bastard!* There were no other possibilities for a homeless, jobless, clueless and penniless woman. He thought of Donovan in his expensive suit, with his designer stubble, touching what belonged to him, and felt rage like never before. He needed to calm down and think clearly. The Anchorage Hotel would be the next place he'd stakeout, but for now he felt the need to let off steam in the only way he could.

He retreated to his mother's house. He couldn't stop thinking about Emily, how she'd abandoned him. *Selfish bitch!* He kicked over a nest of tables and punched his fist into the wall. 'Fucking hotel! That bastard, Donovan.' *How can she disobey me like that?* He'd fed her, clothed her, fucked her and put a roof over her head. *What more did she want? The ungrateful bitch.* He struggled to control himself and stomped down the corridor to the living room.

As Tina heard his footsteps she grimaced at what was to come. A trickle of urine ran down her leg and onto the carpet. Her whole body was defeated. She couldn't take much more, and she could tell by the way Andy stomped towards her that he was in a foul mood.

It was no use, she couldn't escape him or the godforsaken place. She was still bound to the chair and had blisters on her bottom as large as bedsores. Tina's body was frail, and her skin looked as transparent as tracing paper. Her ribs protruded, and she felt numb from the cold. Darkness and damp air surrounded her; she knew she would die alone—and soon—in this dungeon, stinking of mould, piss and shit. Tina had already succumbed to the fact that Andy was a madman, that he'd masked his issues during their relationship and she'd been swayed by his police uniform and luxurious gifts. She knew he was a manipulator and she'd fallen victim to his sadism. She whimpered at the thought of never walking freely in the sun again. *I'm going to die here, by this monster's cruel hand. At least death will free me from this demon . . .*

Tina opened her eyes as she heard the bolt slide across the door. Her heart raced so fast she could hear it thrumming in her ears. The door flung open and Andy stood in the shadows. Tina squirmed in fear of what was in store for her. *Surely the beatings, rapes, mutilation and starvation constitute enough punishment for anyone to take?* But she knew he wouldn't stop. She'd seen the hatred in his eyes. He felt no remorse, he was incapable of it.

Andy came to stand before her. He made her feel small and helpless. He patted her on the head, not gently, and she flinched with every tap. His voice sounded like the devil himself, 'Now, now, good girl. You won't leave, will you?' She couldn't escape even if she tried—and she had tried, anything she could think of. Andy untied the ropes around Tina's wrists and freed her arms from behind her back. Her muscles ached from being restricted and she wiggled her fingers to boost circulation. Andy grinned. 'You're going to put those fingers to good use.' He placed his cock in Tina's hand. She instantly complied and closed her fingers firmly around it, moving her hand up and down in even strokes. She knew not to make a sound; she couldn't speak anyway, the stitches in her lips wouldn't allow it. But Andy couldn't stop her tears. That was something he would never do— unknown to Tina, he liked them.

CHAPTER 25

Donovan walked alongside Emily as they crossed the city square, their shoulders almost touching. The evening was chilly, and the square was packed with people. He felt bad for his actions the previous evening, and ashamed at the way he'd left Emily standing after their kiss. He knew he had to find the courage to tell her the truth, but with minimal damage. *Was that even a possibility?* He had to find the right words and the right time to tell her everything. *Was now the right time?* He'd grown fond of Emily and enjoyed her company, but he didn't know if he could commit to her. Dark secrets from his past haunted him. *Is Emily the one?*

Donovan had been a widower for some time; still he struggled to come to terms with the ordeal. The death of his wife was something no quick fix could resolve. His baggage was more of a burden. He knew it was wrong to mix business with pleasure, but it appeared inevitable under the circumstances. Emily's vulnerability called to him like the sweetest nectar to a bee. Yet again he was trapped by the restraints of someone else's shit—but her innocence was alluring. *Am I letting her get close to me for the right reasons?* When Donovan was alone he thought of Emily constantly, and when he was with her, he struggled to contain himself. He felt a fraud on all levels.

The shops were busy, and the general atmosphere was alive with laughter. Christmas music filled the air. Seconds before 6pm came a countdown, then the Christmas lights shone vibrantly against the night sky. Emily beamed, her face almost childlike. Donovan loved how little things brought her such happiness, it was a remarkable quality that could be put to good use.

It had been years since Emily had celebrated Christmas. Andy hadn't believed in it, he'd said it was nonsense and a waste of good money. Childhood memories rushed forward, of her unwrapping gifts from under the tree, her mother sipping a sweet sherry whilst basting the turkey, and her father watching the same old Christmas movies year after year. *Why did I allow Andy to take over, to ban Christmas?* The thought made her well up, but she sniffed hard so as not to ruin the moment.

Donovan took her hand and pulled her through the crowds. He led her to a horse and carriage; Emily was overcome with excitement. Donovan felt her eyes were so bright they could have lit a football stadium. He was forced to admit to himself that he'd developed feelings for her— it was the first time he'd felt anything for another woman since Helena passed. The feeling was mutual, too; he knew that, he saw it in Emily's eyes. He felt the need to comfort her for as long as he could. He questioned whether it was a charade, as other things were just as prominent in his mind. For now, until he knew for sure which path to follow, he would take things steady.

They climbed into the carriage. It was drawn by two black horses, tinsel twisted into their manes. Emily wore a huge grin, happiness oozing through every pore. Donavon pulled the woollen blanket over their laps and wrapped his arm around her shoulder. Emily leaned into him. As hooves began to clip the cobbles, tears fell down Emily's cheeks.

'What is it?' asked Donovan, concerned.

'No, no, I'm just happy,' she smiled, wiping her nose. 'I don't deserve this.'

'Why would you even think that?'

She didn't answer. Instead, she whispered, 'You're so thoughtful.'

Donovan smiled. 'I just want you to feel good again. I want you to trust me.'

The truth was Emily trusted him unconditionally. And she did feel good, although she couldn't ignore the thought that Donovan only saw her as a victim. She felt small in the big, wide world, insignificant. But, at the same time, she felt more alive than she had in years—and that was down to Donovan. She had a lot to thank him for; he'd become her rock. As the icy wind blew around them, she looked into his eyes. 'Thank you.' Her lip quivered, not from the cold, but from pure emotion.

Donovan playfully rubbed the tip of his nose against hers and she giggled. Emily believed this was the best day ever, a day where she'd felt nothing but light instead of perpetual darkness. She wanted the night to last for eternity, but time had already flown by. On the way back to the hotel they stopped at a cosy-looking café. They ordered a couple of gingerbread lattes—another first for Emily. She tasted the cream with her finger, amused by the miniature gingerbread man on the side of her plate.

Donovan watched her with a smile on his face. *Was this the right moment to tell her about the surveillance? Would there ever be a right time?* He found keeping the secret exhausting; he felt he had to do it now, so they could move on to the next step. *Can she handle the truth?* Donovan took a deep breath as he mulled over words in his head. His mouth felt dry and he took a mouthful of coffee before setting the cup down on the table. 'There's something I need to tell you, Emily, and I need you to hear me out,' he began.

'Okay.' She caught some stray cream from the corner of her mouth with her tongue.

'It's about Andy.'

Emily's smile disappeared immediately. Instinctively, she looked around them, her body tensing. 'Is he here?' she said quietly, her stomach beginning to twist into knots.

'No, he's not here. So, don't worry about that.' Donovan placed his hand over hers in reassurance.

The very mention of her husband's name had caused horrific memories to come hurtling back, memories Emily had tried hard to forget. A chill went down her spine. She noticed that Donovan wouldn't look her in the eye.

'You have to understand, it wasn't my intention . . . ' he continued.

'What wasn't?'

Donovan bit the bullet. He told Emily about his job as a detective, but he insisted that their meeting was entirely circumstantial, even though he'd clearly anticipated meeting Andy. He explained that Andy was the reason he'd taken the property next door.

Emily recoiled, placing her hands in her lap. 'So, you were being nice to me because you wanted to get close to Andy? I'm glad that turned out well for you,' she snapped. She stumbled to her feet so quickly that she knocked her chair over. Pushing her way through the coffee shop, she ran outside.

Emily's head throbbed. She was furious with herself as well as with Donovan. *How could he? Why didn't he mention it before? All men are liars! Why couldn't I see it . . . is there something wrong with me? Am I really that gullible?* She knew the answer; she should have known better. *How could Donovan be interested in someone like me?!* She felt foolish, then remembered their kiss a few days ago. *Did I misread the signals?* Emily wasn't familiar with kindness and she felt confused. She heard Donovan call her name from a few feet away. She didn't look back and increased her pace as she headed to the hotel.

Donovan picked up speed until he was just behind her. 'Please, Emily, just hear me out.'

'I think I've heard enough already. I get it now, I'm just part of your police project. Anything for a result, eh?' She fought to hold back tears, shuffling through the crowd in an attempt to put some distance between them. She felt as though the buildings were closing in on her. She wanted to scream but swallowed it deep down inside.

Donovan didn't think; he grabbed her by the hand firmly enough to stop her in her tracks. Emily froze, her body trembling. Her legs wouldn't move. Immediately, she thought of Andy, of all the times he'd grabbed her. Her breathing became erratic.

Donovan realised his mistake and loosened his grip. He hadn't meant to frighten her, and now he felt an idiot. He said the first thing that came to mind. 'I didn't expect to fall for you.'

Emily met his eyes. She so wanted to believe him. 'I need to think,' she said.

'I'll walk you back,' insisted Donovan. 'It's not safe to be out alone at this time of night.'

They walked to the hotel in an uncomfortable silence. Neither could find the right words to say. Emily's mind was frazzled. She couldn't comprehend how, just minutes earlier, she'd been enjoying the best day she'd had for at least the last eight years of her life, and how it had all turned sour. Donovan had touched her soul, but now those feelings felt tarnished with deceit.

She couldn't stop the thought that she'd been played. She'd finally found the courage to leave her violent husband, only to replace him with a liar—a fraud. The day was ruined. *She* was ruined. Andy had made a damn good job of that.

CHAPTER 26

Keeping to the shadows, silent and unmoving, Andy watched everything unfold as he stood across the road from the Anchorage Hotel. He tried hard to fight his temper at the sight of his wife with Donovan. He despised Donovan's good looks; they angered him, they made him feel inferior. How he wanted to smash his pretty face in.

He noted that Emily looked sad and this pleased him. Her hands were curled into fists and her head was hung low. It didn't take a genius to see that there was tension between the pair. Andy sniggered. *I knew she wouldn't be able to handle things without me.*

Andy couldn't stand the thought of another man touching something that belonged to him. He clenched his fists until his knuckles were white as he thought about his next move. He hadn't anticipated Donovan being with her at this late hour, he'd expected Emily to be alone. 'Goddamn it, fucking whore,' he muttered. The couple moved out of sight into the entrance lobby. He fixed his eyes on the hotel windows and noticed a light come on two floors up. He could make out the silhouettes of two people behind the curtains. He assumed it was Emily and Donovan, and he didn't like it one bit. He chewed the inside of his cheek until it bled. He wanted to run up there and kick the door in, but he knew he had to be patient, despite the adrenaline pumping through his veins.

After an hour the street was empty, except for the odd taxi. Andy continued to lurk in the shadows, glaring up at Emily's window, waiting for some signal that Donovan had left. To his annoyance, nothing happened. He checked his watch; time was marching on, as was the scale of his annoyance. He did the only thing he could do. He went to his mother's house on Benson Lane, his temper at a whole new level.

Tina didn't stand a chance. Her arms and legs were once again bound tightly around the wooden chair, and her limbs were weak. Her body showed the harrowing signs of malnutrition and carnage. Her eyes were only half open, through exhaustion, and her lips were sore and infected. Beads of perspiration were strung along her hairline.

Terror engulfed her as she heard Andy fly through the door. She felt his anger before he even came in the room. He screamed obscenities at her. 'Whore! Slag! Fucking bitch.' Tina quaked with fear but couldn't move. Her eyes wearily followed him across the room as she waited for the assault. Andy punched the wall and the plaster crumbled. He kicked the chair Tina was bound to, knocking it to the ground. Tina lay on the floor, the chair strapped to her body. She was exposed, defenceless.

She saw him lift his boot. There wasn't a thing she could do other than close her eyes and wait for the blow. Andy kicked her repeatedly, each strike hitting its target. Tina whimpered in sheer agony. She was riddled in pain. She heard the terrifying sound of a rib crack and every inch of her body vibrated with shock. She felt bile from her starving stomach rise in her throat, but she couldn't open her mouth to release it. *Choking on it would be better than this* . . . Andy's boot felt like a steel dagger being thrust into her body. The blows were unrelenting. In her mind she thought of nothing but death. She thought that, if there was a god, he'd release her from her suffering. Suddenly, everything turned black. She felt no more.

CHAPTER 27

Donovan stood in the doorway to Emily's room, stricken with guilt. He'd tried to imagine the moment he told Emily the truth, but things hadn't turned out how he'd planned. He'd considered the truth could be damaging, and right now, he was feeling her wrath.

'I just knew you were too good to be true!' Emily ranted.

'You have to listen to me,' he pleaded.

'I trusted you! I'm a fool.'

'Please, Emily, the fault is mine. But I'm not leaving until you listen.'

'Fault?! I'm the fault. Everything is my fault, I get that now! Are you going to punish me?'

Donovan felt as though his heart had been torn into two. 'So, you're saying I'm like him? I'm like Andy? You think I'm going to punish you?'

'I don't know what I am saying. It's just . . . I'm hurt!' she yelled.

Donovan took a step forward and closed the gap between them. Emily was still crying and trying her best to look everywhere but at him. Taking a tissue from his jacket pocket Donovan gently wiped her cheek. 'I never intended to hurt you,' he whispered.

'Well, that went well,' she sobbed.

'Emily, please forgive me. Just listen. You have to listen.'

Deep down, Emily knew Donovan was nothing like Andy. But she was still confused. 'I don't know what came over me,' she cried. It had been so long since she'd yelled, or even spoke her mind. It had actually felt good to let off some steam.

'It's okay to be angry. You've been through enough, that's why I didn't tell you sooner. I thought I was protecting you. I'm an idiot,' he sighed.

'Snap. We're both idiots.'

'I owe you an explanation,' said Donovan.

Over several bottles of red wine they talked through the night. Emily felt ashamed that she'd not given Donovan the chance to explain when he'd shown her such kindness, but everything had seemed like a puzzle where the pieces didn't fit. That was how she summed up her life. Recent events had been a lot to contend with, and she didn't know how much more she could take before she shattered into a thousand pieces, like a chandelier falling from the ceiling. She hadn't known about her husband's secrets until recently, which were hard enough to come to terms with; the fact that he was a suspect and that the victim was still declared a missing person.

Everything she had known about Andy had been a lie, except his temper—that, she knew very well indeed. She wondered where he'd gone to every day over the last year. *Where had he got the money to keep a home running if he was unemployed? Did he have a secret job? Why did he go out wearing his police uniform, and who the hell was Tina Clayton?*

She wanted Donovan to tell her everything he knew; when he obliged, she was shocked, but she wasn't surprised. She felt reassured that Andy was on someone's radar at least, and reasoned that she would never have met Donovan otherwise.

The truth exposed, they huddled together on the couch and watched *Grumpy Old Men*. She felt safe in Donovan's arms. The last of the wine gone, Emily's head felt fuzzy. It was now 2.30a.m. and her eyelids felt heavy. Donovan brushed the side of Emily's face with his fingertips, and suddenly she felt wide awake and stimulated by his sensitivity. She closed her eyes as he gently stroked her, savouring his much-needed touch. He leant into her and brushed his lips softly against hers. She parted her lips to accept him.

She opened her eyes, affection making her yearn for him. This was the moment she'd been waiting for. It all happened so fast. Donovan lifted Emily into his arms and carried her to the bed. All he could think about was her, and what pains he would go to not to hurt her. He straddled her and lifted the sweater over her head before throwing it to the floor. He traces the edge of her bra with his finger, noticing her scars and old, fading bruises.

Emily suddenly felt self-conscious and her body tensed. 'Relax,' Donovan whispered. She did as he suggested and responded to his tenderness. He undid the buttons on his shirt one by one then took hold of Emily's hand and placed it on his chest. Emily felt his heart racing and his firm body, warm. A tingle of pleasure shot through her core and she wanted him like she'd never wanted anything before. Donovan removed his pants and hers; they were naked. His breath was sultry as he left delicate kisses along Emily's thigh. She moaned with pleasure, floating with ecstasy. His touch was as soft as a feather. His lips wandered, and they began to caress her stomach, then her breasts. He eventually put his mouth to hers and the passion inside her ignited as she felt him move gently between her legs. His rhythm was slow, tender, considerate, and Emily melted wistfully into him.

CHAPTER 28

Donovan left early the next morning, knowing he'd taken advantage of Emily when she'd been at her most vulnerable. He berated himself for drinking so much; he should have kept her at arm's length. If he could have kicked himself, he would have. *What an idiot.* He shouldn't have led her on or given her false hope. He wasn't her saviour. He would always be devoted to Helena. Guilt weighed as heavy as a rock.

Cooper was busy following Donovan's lead. He felt sure that Andrew Brooke must have left some clue. When Cooper approached the home of Emily and Andy, his first thought was that, on the outside, the house appeared like any typical family home. The driveway was empty, yet Cooper knocked repeatedly on the door anyway. He peered through the window and noted that the place was a mess. On the mantle stood rows of empty beer cans, lined up like a fairground tin alley. Furniture was turned upside down and a photo on the wall had been defaced; Emily's face had been blacked out with marker pen. Cooper felt a chill. *Boy, does this guy hold a grudge.* He knew this guy had a problem, and not just one involving alcohol. The strength of his temper was apparent in the living room, but to scribble out his wife's face from a photo was just downright eerie.

Clambering over a small gate to the back yard Cooper shuffled through a mound of black bin bags that almost covered the entire yard. On further inspection he saw that they were filled with Emily's clothes and belongings. He lifted the lid on the household bin and found more beer cans and bottles, and a shredded letter. He picked up the document and tried piecing it together; it looked to be the marriage licence of the Brookes. Cooper summed up his findings in three simple words: destruction, chaos, and mess.

Sometime later Cooper called Donovan. 'I tried to locate Andy, to bring him in for questioning about the assault on Emily, but it seems he's disappeared. You want to see the state of his home—it's ransacked. His phone number is dead . . . just watch your back.'

'He can't just vanish,' said Donovan. 'Did you try the bars?'

'You know it's not in my job description to crawl bars.'

'Yeah, sorry man, it's just this has become, well, personal.'

'Got the hots for her, have you? You go, Donovan, you deserve a bit of fun. She carries some baggage, though. Are you ready for that?'

'I was born ready,' laughed Donovan. 'Anyway, Emily's safe. He can't hurt her anymore.'

'You can't take every stray you come across under your wing,' joked Cooper.

'She just needs to be taught the ropes.'

CHAPTER 29

Donovan had seen some things in his time, but he believed that, to gain respect, you had to earn it. He walked down Clover Road with a bag in his hand, handing out sandwiches to the orphaned kids. It had been a few days since he'd last seen them, and he felt a duty to make sure they were okay.

Joanna was thirteen. A scrawny kid, dressed in a cropped top and an old Adidas tracksuit, her hair was matted at the nape and needed a good brush. She was the first to hold out her hand. Donovan noticed that she had a black eye. He didn't press her for information; he already knew, even though he'd tried to put a stop to things, that she had a will of her own. Money was the root of all evil, but it paid for her simple existence. He'd spoken to her about the dangers of soliciting the streets at such a young age, but there was just no talking to some kids. She took the sandwich and gave him a half-smile, then turned down a side street without looking back.

Alfie was the youngest at eleven. He was small for his age, and he had a constant runny nose. He wore a baseball cap back to front and stuttered when he spoke. He'd been teased mercilessly about his speech to the point where he thought it was better to be mute. He bit the sandwich like it was his first and last meal of the day. He threw the plastic wrapper to the ground, nodded his head as a thank you, and set off, like a biker from the Tour de France. His scrawny legs pedalled the old, rusty bike towards the park.

One particular flat on Clover Road held Donovan's attention. He was dealing with his own demons and therefore didn't see a solution until one crossed his mind. It was a secret he couldn't escape.

The door was always unlocked, even though the area was inhabited by the dregs of society. There wasn't much to steal. Today, Donovan wasn't met by the three older girls—the big sisters to Joanna and Alfie—they were out, nowhere to be seen. Donovan knew they'd be working or thieving; they had to eat after all. He called to check on them as often as he could. He felt responsible. His actions had left him with baggage. Donovan needed a resolution, until now he'd thought it impossible. The place was minimal, but it had the essentials: an old cooker that had never been cleaned looked like something from the *House of Horrors*. It looked alive with hideous bacteria. An ash tray overflowed and a pile of old clothes from charity bags had been ransacked and thrown in a corner; it was obvious the bags had been stolen from someone's doorstep. Donovan couldn't complain; kids needed clothes and needs must. These kids had never had a good role model, he was just doing society a favour. He placed the rest of the pre-packed sandwiches on a table and left.

CHAPTER 30

It was just after sunrise on a damp, drizzly, cold Sunday morning. Clare Tinsley was jogging along the river bank, just off Canal Street. She was training for a marathon and her steps matched the beat from her earphones. Something peculiar caught her eye and she stopped in her tracks. She screamed in utter horror as her brain registered that what was laid before her was a dead body.

Her heart raced, and she was scared to take a proper look. She shuffled forwards, gulping nervously, her hand covering her mouth in disbelief as she saw more of the woman's corpse. With trembling hand, she pulled out her mobile and called the emergency services, her voice controlled yet numb in tone. The call over, she scanned the area. There was no one else around. She couldn't look at the mutilated body any longer. She knew she was going to retch and took a few steps backwards.

Time seemed to stand still. She willed the police to hurry up and wrestled over whether she should stay or go. Her instincts told her to run home but her compassion for the stranger caused her to stay. *The police will probably want a statement from me, anyway.* In the distance she could hear sirens. *Please hurry!* When she saw their vehicle, she waved her arms. 'Over here!' she yelled. By the time the officers got to her Clare was sobbing and could only point at where the woman's body had been dumped.

Within minutes, Donovan had arrived at the scene. He thought there was every possibility it was Tina Clayton's body. Immediately, he thought about how he was going to break the news to her parents. Sometimes, he despised this job. He could see the outline of the naked body in the distance, which also made him think of Emily, and how she'd had a lucky escape.

A voice pulled him back to the moment. 'Are you sure you want to do this? What if it's Tina Clayton? You know the family. It will play with your head,' said Cooper.

'I have to. I made the family a promise.' Donovan walked past the tape and towards the crime scene. He could see the trauma the woman had suffered; it was a sickening picture, she was practically unrecognisable. Her scrawny body displayed a protruding spine and a distorted ribcage that could have belonged to someone suffering from anorexia. What was more horrifying, was that her lips had been stitched together meticulously, with blue thread. They were understandably swollen and had become cracked and infected. Rope burns had turned into deep welts at her wrists and ankles, and every inch of her twisted body showed heavy bruising, the vivid purple colour of many a violent assault. Donovan recognised her, even in this state, although he didn't want to admit it to himself. Tina Clayton had suffered a horrendous death and Donovan's instincts told him that Andy Brooke was behind it. When he voiced his concerns in private to Cooper, his colleague questioned whether Donovan's feelings for Emily Brooke were clouding his judgment.

Later, back at the station, forensics confirmed what Donovan already knew, that the mutilated corpse was missing woman Tina Clayton. Finding her dead was not the outcome Donovan had hoped for and he grimaced at the thought of breaking the devastatingly sad news to her family. As they'd been such close friends of his mother's, he knew he had to act quickly; someone was bound to leak the story to the press. Due to the killer's handy work, the station had already given him a nickname: The Stitcher.

Viewing the corpse back at the morgue, Donovan could clearly see just how much Tina had suffered at the hands of the madman who'd held her captive. It wasn't much consolation, but at least she wouldn't suffer any more and her body could be put to rest. The evidence was there in front of him—it was so familiar. Bruising from the sole of a boot, bite marks, things he'd recently seen on Emily; there was a common factor, and that was Andy Brooke. *But why the stitches? What was that all about?* In all his years as a detective he'd never seen anything so brutal and depraved. Donovan wondered if he was even barking up the wrong tree. *Was Andy Brooke, a known wife beater, capable of this type of murder? This much sadism? Maybe Cooper's right, maybe I just dislike Andy so much because of Emily.*

Donovan was out to get Andy, regardless. He'd a hunch about him from the very start, even before he'd got involved with Emily. It's why he'd taken the house next door. But had his own agenda clouded his thinking? He couldn't think straight. He needed air.

Later that day Donovan and Cooper solemnly headed off to break the news to Mr and Mrs Clayton. Donovan felt as though he'd let them down. He'd promised them he would find her, but he hadn't prepared them for finding her like this. Knowing the family made it more difficult. Cooper had insisted on coming along to give moral support, and Donovan was glad of his company. This was something he didn't want to do alone. He didn't want to share the gruesome details of Tina's murder, or the state her body was in when it was found. *What if they asked?* He was overthinking it. During his career he'd often broken news of fatalities to families more times than he liked to recall, but this one left a sour taste in his mouth. Experience had taught him that whether you were a mother, father, grandparent or child, learning that a family member was dead started a process. The first reaction was usually complete disbelief, then a lack of comprehension, followed by tears. Shock then kicked in, and finally, acknowledgement—with a string of questions: *how, when, why?* Donovan had learned over the years to switch off, but this was too close to home. Dealing with grieving families of strangers had become part and parcel of the job but knowing Tina Clayton's parents through his mother's social circle brought an entirely different situation.

'Mr Clayton. Mrs Clayton. I think you both need to sit down.' Donovan blew out his cheeks, there was no mirth in his expression. Mrs Clayton's eyes widened, and her bottom lip began to tremble. She didn't need to hear the words, she already knew what he was going to say, from his drip-white face and hollow eyes. Initially, she declined the offer to sit, and instead paced the floor. All the colour drained from her face.

Before Donovan could tell them anything, Tina's mother collapsed into the arms of her husband, her body continually jerking with the strength of her sobs. Her grief turned into wails. Donovan paused until Mrs Clayton's emotions had subsided a little, then he told them both that they'd found Tina's body. Neither parent took the news well, but it was to be expected. *Of course they're going to take it badly. Tina has been robbed of her life. She was their only daughter, their whole world.*

Mr Clayton's head suddenly flicked up, his brow wrinkled with anger. 'Have you caught the bastard?'

Donovan shook his head. 'I'm working on it.'

'Not quick enough,' growled Mr Clayton.

'I'm really sorry . . .'

'Sorry doesn't bring her back! Bloody police force, sat on their arses, drinking coffee all day long, whilst my baby has been mur…' Mrs. Clayton couldn't finish her sentence. She raised her hands to her temples and wailed.

The look of disgust and hatred on Mrs Clayton's face was something he would never forget. He berated himself over and over for not doing enough to bring Tina home alive. He couldn't find any words, even though deep down he knew it would be impossible to console her at this time. 'I'm sorry for your loss,' he said eventually. 'I promise I will find the person who did this.' With that, Cooper ushered him out of the couple's home.

CHAPTER 31

Donovan drove down the high street and parked outside the Anchorage Hotel. It had been one hell of a day—emotional to say the least. Finding Tina Clayton dead was not the result he'd planned for, and neither was the disappointment from her family at his efforts. He'd been so preoccupied with his own agenda that he'd taken his eye off the ball. His conscience was also pricked by events from the past.

He needed some resolve, to rid himself of all his baggage—some time out. Emily was the answer. He sat in his vehicle for quite a while, the engine off. He felt gripped by the situation and he tried hard to piece his shit together. He thought of Emily, curled up in bed that morning, and felt the burden of false hope weigh heavily. *I can't be the man she wants me to be . . .* Before finding Tina Clayton's body, he'd thought about taking Emily for a meal, somewhere nice and cosy. Beneath his good intentions, the unthinkable lurked in his head. *Can Emily cure my situation?* He needed a distraction from his work and his thoughts.

When he got to Emily's room his jaw dropped and his heart missed a beat. The door was open by several inches. He questioned himself as to whether he'd locked it on his way out. He knew he had; he thought back to the early hours of the morning, when he'd squeezed the key under the doorframe. *Of course I locked it.* Donovan felt a shiver run the length of his spine. He knew something was wrong before he'd even entered the room.

The light was on, and so was the television. Everything seemed to be in place. The bed hadn't been made, though, which he knew was odd. He'd witnessed Emily's domestic discipline—everything had its place and had to be straightened, probably as a result of Andy's controlling habits. He noticed Emily's coat still hanging on the peg behind the door. *She wouldn't leave without it, not in this weather. It's the middle of winter out there.* Slowly, he moved towards the bathroom. It was the only place she could be. Thoughts of what might lay behind the door unnerved him.

He placed his ear to the door. He listened intently and thought he heard a noise. *Maybe she's taking a shower?* Gently, he eased the door open with his foot. The hot tap was running, and steam filled the tiny room. There was no sign of Emily, but it was clear there had been a struggle. Toiletries were strewn across the floor. Donovan jumped to the only assumption he could under the circumstances. *Andy!* He took a deep breath as the realisation swam over him. Emily was missing and in terrible danger. Donovan could feel his heart racing. *This has Andy stamped all over it.* Images of Tina Clayton's mutilated body flashed into his mind. He needed to calm down and think straight, but his body felt tight and anxious as he feared for Emily's safety. He had to rescue her from this madman before it was too late.

Donovan raced to the ground floor and towards reception. *Maybe the receptionist saw something unusual?* Behind the counter was a guy of about twenty. He had dark, greasy hair and was seriously overweight. He had his head stuck in a comic, oblivious to Donovan's urgency.

Donovan slammed the counter to get his attention. 'Emily Brooke. Room 204. Have you seen her?'

'No, man.' The guy shook his head with his eyes half-closed. *Probably from smoking too much weed.*

'Did you hear anything unusual?'

'Nope.' The chubby guy shook his head again, before turning to his comic.

His attitude irritated Donovan, who pulled out his badge from his inside pocket. He waved it in the chubby guy's face. 'CCTV. I want to see it. NOW!'

The guy pointed to the screen. 'Out of order. Sorry, man.'

'Fucking typical!' ranted Donovan. 'Look, did you see anyone enter who wasn't a resident?' He gave a thorough description of Andy.

'Don't think so.'

'Don't think so? Don't know? Oh, what's the fucking use?!' bellowed Donovan through gritted teeth.

Donovan got in his car and screeched away from the hotel. He called Cooper on hands-free, his voice frantic. 'Cooper? He has her, I just know it!'

'Who? Slow down, Donovan,' said Cooper.

'Andy! Andrew Brooke. Emily wasn't in her room. He must have taken her home. I need back up—now!'

CHAPTER 32

Donovan drove like a lunatic, a man possessed. His foot heavy on the accelerator, he ignored red lights. Time was of the essence. The road narrowed, as did his thoughts, and he plunged between moving vehicles before noticing the twinkling lights from a patrol car. He arrived at Andy and Emily's home just as the cops did. He was halfway down the path when the officers battered down the front door. He ran past them, adrenaline flooding through him. He checked every room on the ground floor but there was no sign of Emily or Andy. The place was a mess; it looked like the aftermath of a pub brawl, and he grimaced at the stench of cheap booze and cigarettes.

Donovan ran from one room to another, his eyes scanning every detail of his surroundings. He called out her name, in desperate hope that he may find some clue to her whereabouts. He grabbed the banister and hauled himself upstairs. A dark thought hovered like a black cloud in the sky; maybe he was too late. Maybe she was already dead. One thing was for sure, Donovan wouldn't let Andy get away with it, no matter what. Andy must have left some evidence. When Donovan entered the bedroom he found a scene of destruction. He was used to scenes like this, but he knew by the state of the premises that Andy had crumbled. Whether alcohol or Andy's sadistic needs had won out, Donovan knew he had to think straight if he was to catch him.

A dresser next to the bed had been overturned and a broken lamp lay nearby, its peach shade crumpled. What was left of a glass photo frame was in the far corner and the bed sheets had been dragged from the bed. In the midst of the wreckage one photo stood out like a sore thumb. It remained untouched, which in itself was significant, given the devastation of the rest of the room. Donovan picked it up. It was a photo of Andy as a young boy. He assumed he was with his mother, sat on a doorstep; she had her arm draped over his shoulder. Donovan wondered whether Andy's mother was still alive, and if she still lived at their family home. *Maybe she could shed some light on Andy's hiding places?*

As Donovan entered the bathroom his jaw dropped. Facing him was a message on the bathroom mirror. It looked to have been written in blood. The words said: *the whore is mine.*

Cooper appeared behind him. He put a reassuring hand on Donovan's shoulder, which startled him.

Donovan showed Cooper the mirror. 'Bloody hell, he's a fucking madman,' said Cooper.

'You're not kidding.'

Donovan couldn't tear himself away from the message. Unwanted images crowded his thoughts and he feared the blood was Emily's. 'Get forensics here, and fast,' he muttered.

'On it!' said Cooper.

Donovan ran his hands through his hair. He feared the worst—that Emily was either gravely hurt or already dead. He thought of Helena. *Why can't I keep the women in my life safe?!* He went into the front garden for air. Images of Helena, Emily, Tina Clayton and her parents, clouded his mind. *Am I a bad omen? If only I hadn't got so close to Emily this wouldn't be happening . . . Or would it? Of course it would—Andy Brooke is a sadistic monster.*

CHAPTER 33

Donovan had to take a deep breath before he entered the station. He'd decided he was ready to get it over with, that he couldn't waste time waiting for a warrant. He searched the database for a name and address that he'd come across during his recent searches. He found what he was looking for: Andy Brooke's mother's name. Lilly Brooke. He needed to confirm if she still lived at the same property—the home where Andy grew up.

Lilly Brooke resided on Benson Lane, aged sixty-nine. And, according to records, she was still alive. *That's a start!* He felt pleased with himself; digging into family affairs usually led to something. Every family had skeletons in their closet. *Let's hope I can charm information out of her.* Donovan felt flustered, as though he had suddenly had even more to prove. He rubbed his temples to soothe the headache that was looming. He still felt the weight of his guilt, made heavier by Tina Clayton's brutal murder. *Will Emily be next? Are my instincts accurate enough?* Cooper stepped into the room. Donovan greeted him with a scowl.

'What's up?' asked Cooper.

'You've caught me at a bad time. I'm just about to leave.'

'Just think you should take a look at this first, before you go playing hero.' Cooper waved a clipboard in the air. Donovan paused.

Cooper carried on, 'Forensics ran the blood sample from the bedroom mirror through the database and we have a confirmed match. The DNA is Andy Brooke's. It's his blood. Maybe there's still hope for Emily.'

'Thank fuck for that.' Donovan gave a heavy sigh and felt some relief, but he still feared for Emily's safety. He had to find her—and soon.

'How are you holding up?' Cooper was genuinely concerned for his long-time friend. He'd seen him at his worst, and he didn't want him losing it any time soon.

'I'm pissed off by the whole thing.'

Cooper had seen that look of despair in Donovan's eyes before. He knew him well enough to see right through the cool exterior he projected.

'Look, Donovan, you're not going to like what I have to say, but you're way too involved with Emily Brooke. For all we know she could be taking a walk in the park. It's clouding your judgment and it's not that long since . . . well, you know.' Cooper dropped his voice into a whisper. 'The drunk driver. We can't play vigilante, if you get my drift, can we?'

'Why are you bringing that up? We agreed that subject is taboo,' snapped Donovan. He didn't want to relive his mistakes of the past at that moment.

Cooper knew he'd overstepped the mark, but he genuinely wanted Donovan in sound mind. 'I believe that the murder of Tina Clayton is a separate issue. Any husband would be pissed if their wife had run off. Even though Andy is a wife beater it doesn't mean he's a killer. He's just an alcoholic with a very controlling personality. Why don't you let someone else take over the case while you sort your head out?'

'You're kidding me, right?!'

Cooper shook his head disapprovingly. He knew Donovan's stubborn streak well. There was no point pressing him further, even if he also knew that he'd have to pick up the pieces, just as he had done before. 'Anyway,

I've brought the info you requested, plus more.' Cooper unpinned the sheets from the clipboard and handed them over. Donovan just dropped them on his desk. He didn't need to look at them, he'd already found what he was searching for. He didn't have time to hang around for another of Cooper's therapy sessions, even though he knew his friend had his best interests at heart. He had a duty as a detective to serve justice. Andy's bloody message on the bathroom mirror jumped back into his mind. He walked out the door without saying another word.

Cooper wouldn't let things drop. Like a puppy at his heel, he followed Donovan through the station. 'There's more info in there about Tina Clayton to support what I'm telling you. You need to take a look before you go headhunting,' he pressed.

'More? What is it?' Donovan's patience was wearing thin. 'Go on, tell me. What is it?'

Cooper took hold of his friend's arm and brought him to a standstill. 'It's more complicated than you think, so get Andy and Emily Brooke out of your mind for one moment and focus. Evidence from another unit suggests we may well have a serial killer in the area, a.k.a The Stitcher. Analysts have found a connection that may relate to Tina Clayton.'

Donovan allowed himself to be ushered into a room further down the corridor. Maybe his emotions had compromised his rationale. *Have I really been that hasty?* There was a white board in a central position in the room. It was covered in photos of assaulted and missing women within a twenty-mile radius of their location—structured in relevant timelines. *Eleven women in a two-year period . . . someone has been busy.*

The evidence showed a clear picture of how the murders had escalated over the years. They began with assaults and beatings, then rape. Then came murder, with its own unique stamp. Donovan analysed each of the photos. What stood out, apart from the familiar blue stitches in three of the victim's lips, were the victims' clear similarities. It was staring him in the face. All the confirmation he needed; the photo evidence was clear as the nose on his face.

Each victim displayed the same pattern of bruising or damaged tissue: an imprint of a boot, which looked very much like the standard issue footwear of a cop. *Why had Cooper not seen that?* It was clear that Tina Clayton was not Andy Brooke's first victim. *The Stitcher . . .* The realisation railroaded him; his instincts had been on point, yet the case was far bigger than Donovan had imagined. He couldn't and wouldn't hang around any longer. He had to follow his hunch about the address on Benson Lane.

'Where are you going?' asked Cooper.

Donovan rolled his eyes, irritated that Cooper couldn't see the obvious. 'Sometimes, you're a total muppet. Think about it. Check out the boot print, the shape of the sole. It's a cop!'

'What do you mean, a muppet? Cheeky git!'

'Oh, for God's sake! I've told you this already. It's Andy Brooke, he's The Stitcher, and now he's got Emily.'

Donovan turned to walk away but Cooper persisted. 'Donovan, will you just listen, you stubborn shit? There's no easy way of telling you this, but there's another team that's been brought in. They're taking over the investigation.'

'On what grounds?' Donovan snapped. *Why isn't Cooper listening to me or taking me seriously?* Donovan's instincts were screaming loud and clear: *follow your gut!* His gut told him that the serial killer was Andy Brooke, and that Emily was in danger. Nothing or no one was going to stand in his way.

'You've got to understand—I'm concerned, and I know it's become personal. This thing you have about Brooke . . . what if you're wrong about him? I have your back, mate, but I'm worried that you're letting your personal feelings get in the way, and I don't want to see you screw up a second time. I think your judgment has flown out the window.'

'My judgment is just fine.' Donovan scowled at Cooper before he left the office. He knew in his heart that this had Andy Brooke's stamp all over it, much like his boot prints on the bodies of his victims. Donovan wanted Cooper on board; he had no idea why his friend couldn't see what was blatantly obvious. He also knew that putting a new team together meant a lot of red tape and paperwork. There wasn't time for that, the clock was ticking, and Emily was in danger. Donovan felt as though it was his duty to help her. He needed her as much as she needed him. All that mattered was saving Emily, and he wasn't going to waste another moment standing idly by. He had to find her.

CHAPTER 34

Emily felt petrified. She didn't recognise the run-down property on Benson Lane as Andy marched her through the front door, her arm twisted painfully up her back. Andy scanned the street, desperate not to be noticed. Emily's whole body trembled, and her legs felt like they could give way at any moment. 'I'm sorry,' she whispered through muffled sobs. Even though she knew she had nothing to be sorry for, her only thought was trying to save her life.

'You fucking will be. Sorry doesn't match the crime,' Andy growled. He slammed the door shut behind them with his foot, blocking out the light from the street. There wasn't even a light-bulb hanging from the ceiling in the passageway, and barely any light seeped through the small glass window. Her eyes tried to adjust to the darkness as he pushed her on further. The only sound was his heavy breath against her neck.

Andy ushered her forward forcefully, thrusting her into what she took to be a living room. The room was even darker than the hallway; the curtains were drawn, banishing all-natural light. A foul smell hovered in the damp air—rotten, like an old folk's home, but amplified by decay. The putrid stench of stale urine and vomit lined her nostrils and she retched. Despite the darkness Emily could see the outline of a chair in the middle of the room. Tears rushed to her eyes and she feared what was to come. She started to sob, though she knew Andy was unlikely to sympathise.

Andy shoved her with the palm of his hand, forcing her to stumble onto the ground. He laughed at her vulnerability.

She put her hands over her ears, in a bid to block out his cruel taunts. 'You fucking whore,' he spat, 'making a mockery of me.' His voice echoed around the empty room.

Emily had nowhere to run. *I'm never going to escape him . . .*

She heard his feet shuffling across the carpet. He struck a match and lit two candles, but they did little to relieve the darkness. 'Please don't hurt me,' she begged. She curled up in a ball, sobbing, too afraid to look up at him. It was her way of protecting herself against his fists and boots. She knew him too well. She wasn't going to get off lightly, if at all.

Images of how he was going to kill her flashed in her mind and her panic rose to another level. *What the hell is this place? Why does it smell of death and decay? Oh, lord, I'm going to die in this cesspit by his barbaric hand.* Andy's voice brought her back to the moment as she quaked on the floor.

'Fuck! You're my wife. You belong to me. Why, oh why the fuck did you do it? And with that tosser, Donovan!' he ranted.

Emily didn't dare answer back, she didn't want to provoke him further. She knew from previous experience that it was better to surrender to his needs. Her head screamed with contradictions that she wasn't brave enough to share. *Donovan is no tosser! He's kind, caring, and more of a man than you'll ever be.* Though she faced a beating, and maybe even death, Emily recalled Donovan's kindness at the mention of his name. She was thankful that she'd escaped Andy's clutches, even if it was for just a short time. She considered herself fortunate to have felt something other than hate. Donovan had given her a strength that hadn't been there before she'd met him.

It was this strength that saw her get to her feet. Years of repressed energy came to the fore. She stood inches away from Andy's face. 'You're a bully. Do what you will, you violent arsehole. I'm already broken, I have nothing more to lose. No matter how many times you punish me, I will never, ever love you. I hate you!'

Andy shook, incandescent with rage, as she spoke. He let out a growl like a wild animal. His teeth bared, he lunged forward and grabbed Emily by her shoulders. Like a bowling ball knocking over a pin, he overpowered her, pinning her to the ground with her two arms above her head. He used his weight to straddle her petite body. She was faced with his twisted smirk, and she could smell the familiar stench of alcohol.

His face next to hers, she could feel the spit from his words and his sour breath on her face. 'I gave you everything. Why?' he sneered.

Emily wanted to scream: *you gave me nothing but physical and mental pain!* But there was no point, so she kept her mouth shut. He leant forward and kissed her lips before sniffing at her hair, savouring her scent. He tried nuzzling into her. She felt bile rise in her throat and had an urge to vomit. She tried struggling against his restraint, but he was too strong. She turned her head away, tears escaping down her cheeks. *Don't show fear, that's what he wants.* But she couldn't help it.

To her disgust, Andy ran his tongue across her cheek, mopping up her tears. Emily held her breath; she felt dehumanised. *I can't take any more . . .*

'You belong with me,' he whispered in her ear.

CHAPTER 35

44 Benson Lane looked to have been abandoned—it was a property that would only appeal to squatters. The windows were filthy, and it needed some serious repair work. Donovan felt it would be even more of a hovel inside. He clenched his fists and knocked on the door several times, hoping that Lilly Brooke would open up. But she didn't. He moved down the narrow passageway at the side of the house to access the back yard. Unsurprisingly, the garden was overgrown, and clutter was piled up in mounds. Amongst the debris sat an old shopping trolley, which was full of rubble and discarded trash. It didn't look like anyone had lived there for years. *Maybe Lilly Brooke isn't capable of maintaining her own home and garden?*

To Donovan's annoyance, he found both doors locked, and every curtain drawn shut. He knew Andy was in there, given that his car was parked outside, the hood of his engine still warm to the touch. Donovan figured he had no alternative. He took off his jacket, wrapping it around his hand. He punched through a small glass panel in the back door, searching for a latch or a key. It was no use; he couldn't reach. He had no warrant, so he did what he thought was best. He called Cooper.

'What mess have you got yourself into now?' said Cooper with a heavy sigh.

Donovan's words came quick and fast. Finally, it dawned on Cooper that Donovan's theory may just add up. He felt a little shame for doubting his friend. He couldn't leave Donovan to his own devices, and so, just seven minutes later a fleet of squad cars arrived at the property.

The team battered down the front door. Dust floated in the air and the stench of decay hit the officers hard, lingering in their nostrils, and they instinctively covered their noses. Donovan raced to find Emily; following the sound of her distressed sobs he rushed through the narrow hall to the living room. He held his hand up to the response team behind him, swung open the door and lunged forward.

Donovan suddenly stopped in his tracks. Emily was curled up in a corner, quaking, her clothes ripped apart. Blood trickled from the corner of her mouth. To his relief, she was alive and there was no sign of blue stitches in her lips. Her frail, timid state caused Donovan's anger to bubble inside.

Andy was stood over Emily with a leather belt in his hand.

'You're a bastard,' Donovan spat.

'Well, she was already dead below the waist. We hadn't had sex for years, so I took her—hard. She begged for it. It felt good.' Andy smirked as he taunted Donovan.

Donovan's stomach churned, and his temper flared. He recalled the state in which he'd found Emily all those weeks ago. *To now find her like this . . . what the hell is wrong with this guy?* He tried to rise above Andy's comments.

'I'm a man. I've got needs.' Andy gave Donovan a wide grin.

'So has a rabid dog, and there's only one solution to that—have it put down!' snapped Donovan. He felt the need to wipe the smug smile from Andy's face. In that instant, all his policing experience and thoughts of official procedure flew out the window. He ignored the fact that he should subdue Andy rather than attack him. His temper had escalated to another level; like steam escaping from a boiling kettle he took a swing at Andy.

His knuckles bounced off Andy's jaw. He felt that the pain gyrating through his knuckles was worth it. Andy simply shook his head, not fazed by the punch whatsoever, the grin still on his face. He swung the leather belt in retaliation; it caught Donovan on the shoulder. Donovan flinched and felt his skin sting. Spotting weakness, Andy followed this with a string of punches. Donovan didn't hesitate to return the favour.

Moments later, a yell came from Cooper, who had reached the doorway. 'What the hell are you playing at?! Just make an arrest or let the guys take over! You're going to jeopardise everything.' The rest of the team moved on hearing Cooper's rant. The force's code of practice flashed through Donovan's mind and his bruised fists stilled as the team moved forward and swiftly intervened. Cooper took hold of Donovan by his lapels, in an attempt to drag him to his senses. 'You need to calm your temper,' he chastised.

The team easily overpowered Andy and cuffs were on his wrists in seconds. As he was hauled away, he shouted, 'Emily? You belong to me. Forever!' His madness echoed around the room.

Emily had had her fingers in her ears the whole time Donovan and Andy clashed. Her husband's words rattled around her head like a bird in a cage. *I'll never be rid of him, not ever. Regardless of whether he's behind bars or not, he'll always be in my head.* She continued to cower and shake with fear, despite Andy's removal. Her skin showed the impact of his belt.

Donovan knelt next to her and he gently stroked the side of her face with his fingertips. 'It's over, you're safe,' he soothed. Once again, her saviour, she threw her arms around his shoulders and crumpled into him. Unable to contain her tears, she knew Andy's memory would follow her like a dark and gloomy shadow for all eternity.

Donovan guided her to an ambulance waiting outside. She assured the paramedics that she was fine, but Donovan wasn't convinced. 'Cooper, can you keep an eye on her while I check the place out?'

Cooper nodded. 'Always the babysitter,' he mumbled under his breath.

CHAPTER 36

Donovan searched the property room by room. There were cobwebs from ceiling to floor throughout. Behind one door things were more sinister than he'd anticipated. To his horror, a decaying corpse was laid on the bed. Donovan put a hand over his mouth—the putrid stench of rotting flesh swamped the air.

Later, it was confirmed that the body was that of Lilly Brooke. She'd been neatly positioned, with care and consideration, on top of a dusty, once-pink blanket—fully clothed. There were signs of mutilation and stitches through her lips, although they had since been removed. She wore red heels, which had matched the colour of her dress; the shoes were a couple of sizes too small and had been secured to her feet. On her left hand her fingers had been severed but then stitched back on with the familiar blue thread. She looked to have endured many afflictions and monstrous mutilations.

Information later showed that Andy Brooke, her only known son, had been claiming her disability cheque, even after her death. The coroner's report concluded that Lilly Brooke had died as a result of starvation. At some point her wrists and ankles had been bound, and she had broken bones throughout her body. Forensics confirmed the injuries had been sustained before death, which included two cracked ribs and a fractured pelvis. It was also established that semen, which matched the DNA of Andy Brooke, was found in and around her body; intercourse occurring after her death.

Donovan wondered if Andy's sadistic nature was a trait or as a result of learned behaviour. He deduced that it probably stemmed from a few factors. One thing was certain: Lilly Brooke suffered terribly at the hands of her son. The bond between mother and child, Donovan felt, should never be broken. Something had shattered this relationship, or maybe it was doomed from the very start—had Andy paid his mother back for the hunger he endured during his childhood; after all, Lilly herself has been starved to death. Andy had witnessed his mother sell her body on numerous occasions and had formed the belief that women had no respect for themselves. Perhaps seeing his mother subjected to violence on a daily basis at the hands of clients, boyfriends or pimps could have turned Andy into pure evil. One thing was certain, Brooke had no empathy towards women. He was a serial killer and would be forever known as The Stitcher.

CHAPTER 37

Emily waited in a private room at the station after refusing hospital treatment. She had no desire to be poked and prodded again. She didn't believe Andy would be imprisoned. *He has a knack for getting out of situations.* When she found out about his mother and realised that everything she knew about him was a lie she struggled to believe it. *So, he wasn't an orphan . . .* Emily had never known Lilly Brooke existed. *To think Andy managed to keep that a secret all these years. And murdering and mutilating his own flesh and blood . . . leaving her laid there in the home he grew up in, just a few miles down the road . . . that's something else. What kind of monster is he?!*

She conceded that she knew very little about the man she'd married. Everything felt surreal, like she was looking at someone else's life, not her own. She anxiously picked at her cuticles until they bled, not that she was aware. She mulled over her disastrous life and couldn't see a light at the end of the tunnel. *This will haunt me forever.* She focused on the fact that everything was over. *If what Donovan said is true, Andy will be banged up for a long time. I won't have to cower or hide in the darkness any more.*

Memories of her torment would always be there but, as Donovan assured her, time was a great healer. She wished she had his confidence.

'How you doing?' A woman stood in the doorway and Emily jumped, startled.

'Fine,' Emily answered.

'Would you like a tea or coffee?' The officer nodded whilst speaking, as though willing Emily to say yes.

'Coffee, please.' *What the hell's wrong with me? I'm not fine, I'm sick to the back teeth. Why do we, as a species, always pretend everything is okay? And why did I say yes to a coffee? My hands aren't even steady enough to hold the damn cup!*

The sound of the clock ticking began to get on her nerves. *I need to get out of here. Anywhere but here . . .* Her chest felt tight. *I can't breathe!* The room began to spin. By the time the officer returned Emily was in meltdown. She was rocking back and forth on her chair, her fingers entwined in her hair, trying to pull it out. 'I can't do this anymore. I can't take it!' she wailed.

'You're safe now, sweetie,' the officer soothed, but Emily had heard enough. She'd had as much as she could cope with for one day. She put her fingers in her ears to drown out the woman's voice and shut out the world.

CHAPTER 38

The experiences of both Lilly and Andy Brooke played on Donovan's mind. *Who knows what Lilly endured before her death?* It seemed obvious to him that Lilly's lifestyle had affected her son's behaviour, which brought Donovan to a conclusion. *Kids need a mother . . . a good mother.* He thought about Helena and how they never had chance to plan a family, about how their choices had been cruelly stripped away.

He knew from the first moment he'd met her that Emily would make a great mother. He thought she'd be a good role model; that she would nurture, cherish and love a child. After Helena died, he felt as though he'd lost himself, like he'd sunk to the deepest part of the darkest ocean, not able to catch a breath nor find his way to the surface and to normality.

Donovan never brought the drunk driver who'd killed his wife to justice. He'd enforced his own punishment, and with that action came consequences. *Is it guilt that burdens me, following that fateful day? Do I even have a heart?* When Donovan sought out Sarah Morris the situation got completely out of hand, to catastrophic proportions. Fuelled by grief and anger, he held her accountable for the murder of his wife. His emotions clouded his judgment and caused him to discard his professionalism. The outcome wasn't what he'd anticipated, if he even had any prior thought about his actions.

He recalled the events as if he was watching a recording. Sarah Morris had lived in a tiny flat on Clover Road for years—a single mother with a string of kids to a few absentee fathers. When Donovan walked up to her door on that fateful day, he took a deep breath. He told himself that, if he actually faced his dead wife's killer, instead of watching her from afar, he could find closure and move on.

How wrong could I have been? He'd knocked and knocked without getting any answer, yet he could hear that someone was in. He tried the door, which was unlocked, and crept inside the hallway. A musty stench surrounded him. The place was filthy. A table in the room to his right was covered in discarded takeaway boxes, which looked like they were forming their own eco-system. The furniture was old and worn.

He could hear whimpers coming from behind a door that he guessed led to the kitchen. They sounded like they came from a child. The door was bolted and had to be opened from the hallway. There was a bolt at the top and another at the bottom. He moved forward to investigate. *Why are these kids locked away? Who would do that?* Before he had time to slide the bolts aside, he heard high heels coming towards him as they clicked along the tiled floor. He quickly turned and came face to face with Sarah Morris.

Her head hung low as she staggered through the doorway, drunk as a lord. To him, she looked like a crack whore and his mind ran amok. He watched her fumble in her shoulder bag for a cigarette, completely oblivious to his presence. She swayed from side to side, disorientated, as she struggled to remain upright. Smudged mascara framed her bloodshot eyes. *Has this drunk not learned a thing? Is taking a life not enough for her? Has she no shame, respect—or even guilt—about what she has done?* He'd lost everything he deemed important, yet this woman still had the audacity to put alcohol to her lips and pour it down her throat.

Donovan couldn't help himself. His temper flared, and his thoughts turned dark. His wife's image burned the back of his eyes.

After several moments of drunken stupor, Sarah finally noticed Donovan. She stumbled backwards a few steps. Her eyebrows raised, and she tried to form a sentence. 'Who . . . who . . . what you want?' she slurred.

Donovan felt repulsed by her. *What a drunken mess. It's disgusting that she's left her children locked in a room. What if there'd been a fire? What kind of mother is she? Certainly not a good one, by the looks of things.*

He saw the half-bottle of cheap vodka protruding from her jacket pocket and a rage came over him, the likes of which he'd never felt before. His wife, the love of his life, was dead and gone, never to return, while this waste of space drank herself to oblivion—uncaring and unrepentant. He could drink the city's supply of alcohol and still he wouldn't be able to forget; his grief never ceased.

It happened so quickly. It was like a fog absorbed him, temporarily blinding his rational mind. He grabbed Sarah by the arm and pushed her forcefully on to the sofa. *If she wants vodka, she can damn well have it.* Pinning her down with the weight of his body, he prised the bottle from her pocket. He tilted her head back; she was too drunk to put up much of a struggle.

He unscrewed the cap from the bottle and forced the clear liquid down her throat until every drop was consumed. Her natural gag reflex kicked in and she retched a couple of times, but she couldn't shake him off. At one point, she gulped back her vomit along with the alcohol.

Donovan was unaware that he'd lost control, or that he was capable of such hatred. He saw himself as righting a wrong, the simple actions of a grieving husband; he wasn't a monster like Andy Brooke. He didn't let Sarah budge, however much she wriggled beneath him. He continued to hold her down—only now, with his hand over her mouth and nose.

It didn't take long for her limbs to stop flailing. She became unresponsive, her skin taking on a blue tinge as her blood pressure dropped. Her breathing became shallower and shallower until she had no fight left. Her life disintegrated before him.

Within seconds the fog lifted, and the realisation of his actions hit him. He jumped away from her, horrified, and began pacing the floor. He rubbed his temples. *What the hell have I done?* He cursed to himself, panic-stricken.

He could still hear crying from behind the door. *I can't think straight, I've got to get out of here . . .* He left the building, worrying whether someone had seen him. He sat in his car in a daze, thinking through his options and questioning his morals. Taking out his mobile with shaking hands he called Cooper. 'I've messed up big style,' he cried down the phone.

Twenty minutes later Cooper was at his side. 'Shit, Donovan, you should have left well alone,' he chided. Donovan couldn't speak; he was in a state of shock. Everything seemed surreal. 'Look, you need to get a grip or you're going down for this.'

'What the hell have I done? I just . . .' Donovan buried his face in his hands.

'Let me think.' Cooper wasn't going to see his best friend go to prison. He felt a duty to him and Helena; he'd promised her on her death bed that he would look out for Donovan, no matter what—but he hadn't expected to clear up a murder as part of that promise. Eventually, together, they managed to clean the scene, getting rid of any evidence and DNA that could link Donovan to being in the flat. The kids remained locked away; even though they continued to cry, the pair couldn't afford to be seen. They kept their voices to a whisper for the same reason.

Cooper came up with a plan. It was difficult to keep Donovan focused, but somehow, they managed to pull it off. They staged an accident; stripping Sarah of her ID, they dumped the body in a place where the homeless often gathered. They made it appear as if she was just another drunk of no fixed abode who had been unfortunate enough to die of consumption. During their time in law enforcement they'd become familiar with the statistics that showed alcohol-related deaths were common amongst the homeless—accounting for over a third of deaths. The police weren't going to be overly interested in another waster found dead in the gutter; homeless drunks and drug users weren't worth pursuing with tax payers' money.

With any trace to him eradicated Donovan had another issue: the kids behind the bolted door. He couldn't leave them to starve, but neither could he inform social services— the risk was too high.

He returned to the flat with Cooper; they found five kids home alone behind the door. They were dirty and hungry. Donovan looked at their little faces and guilt hit him. He'd left them motherless. He was to blame. It was clear Sarah had been a shitty mother and that they didn't have much of a childhood—after all, who locked their kids up to go partying?—but now they had no one. He sat them on the sofa, explained they were police officers and that they'd come to break the news that their mother had run away, never to return. Innocent, and clearly used to hardship, the children accepted his version of events with little reaction; Donovan was surprised at how easily they'd believed him.

He would carry the burden for eternity. Donovan couldn't justify his actions and he felt remorse daily. He convinced himself that what had happened with Sarah Morris was payback, yet most nights he woke with a start, sweat on his brow, as he relived her last moments. He could still feel how she had struggled under his hand. *Am I a monster, or did she just get what she deserved? An eye for an eye . . .* It was all well and good turning the other cheek, but it wasn't as easy to forget.

CHAPTER 39

Andrew Brooke had been left alone in an interview room for the best part of an hour. On a shelf in the corner was a digital recorder and a small CCTV camera that was focused on the room. He'd been searched and had his mobile phone confiscated; tech support had quickly confirmed that it held more than forty images of his victims; seemingly, a way for Andy to revisit his memories of each one.

In total, seven victims were linked to Andy Brooke, their bodies found in the back-garden debris of the house on Benson Lane. Buried in shallow graves, each woman bore a common denominator—their lips had all been stitched with blue thread. The photos also showed physical similarities between the victims; each had the same shade of hair, the same build, and all were wearing the colour red before their murder.

Andy Brooke didn't ask for a lawyer, although he knew the system. As he was escorted from room to room, and then to his cell, he wore a psychotic grin across his face. His fingers would casually strum tunes on a table and he gave off a 'not a care in the world' attitude. A uniformed constable constantly watched his every move.

Donovan took a deep breath before he entered the interview room. Andy Brooke was a first-rate bastard in his eyes, but he needed to put his personal feelings to one side. He pulled up a chair across from him and turned on the tape. Andy was read his rights, and he complied with the routine questions: name, date of birth, etc. Eventually, he couldn't help himself. 'Enjoy it, did you? Putting your cock in my wife,' he sneered to Donovan, before laughing like a madman.

Donovan muttered something under his breath. He was finding it more and more difficult to keep hold of his temper. He couldn't lose it now, there were still the nameless bodies to identify that had been found in the shallow graves.

'Warm and wet, was she?' Andy mocked again.

Donovan cleared his throat, composed himself, and carried on. He stuck to the routine. Questions had to be answered and he wasn't going to let Andy play mind games with him. He bit his tongue and put his best poker face on. He just wanted it over and done with, he still had his own shit to deal with.

Cooper interrupted, and Donovan left the room. 'What's up?' Donovan asked when they were outside.

'Forensics has identified four out of the five bodies found in the shallow graves at Lilly Brooke's residence.' He handed over a list of names and photographic ID.

- Abigail Stout, age 32
- Michelle Bishop, age 35
- Clara Donald, age 27
- Deborah Galloway, age 31

'What about the fifth body?' asked Donovan.

'No clue.'

It has been established that each victim had suffered serious sexual assault and torture before their death. Despite intense interrogation Andy refused to give up the name of the fifth victim. Donovan felt some sadness that the poor woman could not be put to rest, that family members may still have been searching for her. But police work was often like that; sometimes, the answer everyone wanted never came.

Andy Brooke was charged with the kidnap and assault of his wife, as well as several murder charges, including that of his own mother, Lilly Brooke. His DNA matched that found on Tina Clayton and the corpses of Abigail Stout, Michelle Bishop, Clara Donald and Deborah Galloway. The database also tied him to a rape in an alleyway; the victim's name: Carla Walker. Andrew Brooke, also known as The Stitcher, was caught bang to rights.

It was hard to believe for those watching that he was actually being interrogated for murder. Throughout, his face appeared like a child's at a fairground as they won their first goldfish. The whole procedure didn't bother him in the slightest. It was like his sanity had been stripped away like cheap wallpaper. The police had in their clutches a sexual sadist. Andy would not find himself at liberty any time soon.

CHAPTER 40

In a foul mood to start with, Donovan felt further irritated. He hated loose ends. The final victim remained nameless and Andy Brooke's twisted smirk just infuriated him.

Donovan also had loose ends of his own. Emily sat in reception at the station; she was a wreck. She thought that if she had to endure one more interview she may lose control—all because she hadn't really known the man she'd been married to. She dissected every aspect of their time together. *What a fool I've been.* The words 'serial killer' rolled around her head like a marble in a cup. *How could I have been so blind?* Every aspect of her marriage had been a lie. Even though she despised Andy for what he'd done to her, she felt cheated and ashamed that she'd been totally clueless.

Donovan pulled up in front of the hotel. Emily had said very little since her ordeal. She'd looked more fragile with every mile they'd driven. She felt as though she was cursed, haunted by misery. Donovan knew she was vulnerable and easily to manipulate; he considered whether he was doing the right thing, but he couldn't visualise another outcome however hard he tried.

Cooper doesn't have to know everything. Besides, it's not him left holding the fort. He narrowed his eyes at Emily. 'Are you alright?' he asked. She nodded. Donovan felt uncomfortable with his thoughts. *Be strong, Donovan!*

In Emily's hotel room Donovan insisted she packed the few belongings he'd bought for her. He held back from giving her an explanation and Emily wondered where they were going. *Somewhere exciting? Romantic?* She didn't mind where they went, as long as it was far away from the here and now. After everything that had happened, she was happy to follow his lead. She didn't even bother folding the items, she just stuffed them into a carrier bag.

'Let's go,' said Donovan.

CHAPTER 41

Yorkshire was typically unpredictable—promising one minute, then dismal. A freak hailstorm pounded surfaces furiously and your breath came out as freezing mist. Despite this, the tips of daffodils prevailed; with spring in the air it made Donovan think of Emily as an innocent little lamb. *Can I really lead her to slaughter?* He was sick of mulling it over—if she could survive Andy and his secrets, his was nothing in comparison. She was ready, and the answer to his hell.

Night after night he'd considered his options but knew opportunities like this didn't arise very often. Donovan needed closure and couldn't see any other solution. He couldn't come to terms with the loss of his wife; he hadn't grieved properly, and he still felt accountable for his subsequent actions. *Sometimes everything happens for a reason.* He did have feelings for Emily, but they weren't strong enough to replace his wife's memory. The battle in his mind between guilt and burden wouldn't let him move on. He felt as though doing so would be a dishonour to Helena.

He had to put the past behind him, wipe the slate clean—maybe then he could sleep for a whole night without any disruption. It hadn't been his intention, when he'd first spoken to Emily across that fence, that she would be the one, nor was it his intention to feel such empathy for her.

He couldn't keep up the pretence, it was soul destroying. Neither could he give those children what they wanted and needed. The terrible guilt from leaving them motherless was all he could think about, it consumed him every day.

He'd taken away their mother with his own hands and had discarded her like trash. He couldn't live with that.

He'd visited the flat that very day, in the early hours. He was greeted by a cold air that hit him like a smack to the face. The kids were huddled together, asleep on the sofa. It pained him to think of the help and guidance they needed, which he was struggling to give. The littlest one, Joanna, woke up whilst he stood there, watching them. She rubbed her eyes and muttered, 'Molly from down the road made fun of me.' Her eyes brimmed with tears and she begged Donovan to stay. 'Are you my dad?' she whispered.

Donovan swallowed the lump in his throat. 'No. You know I'm just supervising you whilst your mum's away.'

'Can I call you Dad?'

Donovan could only shake his head. The heat from her questions was making him uncomfortable.

Joanna blinked as she tried to stay awake. 'When's Mum coming home? I want to be like the other kids.'

Donovan felt guilt like a wrought-iron bar through his heart. He didn't often see such innocence in tough street kids. He couldn't give her any answers, just more lies so that his misdemeanour remained a secret. *This whole thing is a pain in the ass!*

'Please find my mum or ring her. I'm sure she's got a phone. Please tell her that I want her to come home.'

'I'll try, but I can't promise anything.' He gave the little girl a smile, but his eyes showed something far more sinister. He had that same fight or flight feeling he'd had when faced with Joanna's mother. *I've got to get out of here, and fast.* He dropped the bag of groceries on the table and quickly left, Joanna's words playing havoc in his mind. He needed to find a permanent answer.

CHAPTER 42

Packed and ready to go, Emily and Donovan left the hotel room. Emily wondered if this was the first chapter of her new life. As they reached the ground floor, she noticed that Donovan was not his usual self. He was unnaturally quiet. *Maybe he doesn't want to give the surprise away? Perhaps recent events have caught up with him. He's probably mentally exhausted.* She knew that feeling well.

Pausing at the reception in the lobby, Donovan slid the room key across the counter towards the familiar fat guy, who was too intrigued with Candy Crush on his phone to notice their departure. That's when it hit Emily: she hadn't realised that she wouldn't be coming back. She considered, now that Andy was banged up, that Donovan was taking her home. For a moment Emily couldn't breathe; at the thought of home. She wasn't ready to enter the place that held horrifically painful memories. *Maybe I should sell it, and that way I can pay Donovan back what I owe him. He has been generous and footed the bill for my digs.*

Yet something didn't feel right. Donovan seemed agitated, distant. Emily couldn't put her finger on what the problem was, but as she trusted him, she followed his lead, like a lost puppy. Wherever they were going, she was with him, that was all that mattered. She'd been touched by kindness instead of madness, and she was grateful for everything he had done. In fact, she didn't really know what she would have done without him.

As he started the engine the radio blasted. Donovan hit the accelerator hard, tossing the vehicle around every corner like a Formula One driver. It wasn't his usual manner; Emily hadn't seen this erratic side of him before and she felt unnerved. He tapped his fingers on the steering wheel, glaring at the road before him. Emily found the lack of conversation uncomfortable and her instincts were suddenly on full alert. She turned her head towards him and, for one moment, she saw a glimpse of Andy.

She gave herself a talking to and conceded that her head was all over the place. Still something niggled her, she just couldn't pin point what. She turned the radio's volume down and asked Donovan outright, 'Is everything okay?'

'Fine,' he replied dismissively, his eyes never leaving the road. Emily could tell this was a lie, it was written in the furrow of his brow and the intensity of his glare. She didn't like it. She stared out of the window at the passing traffic, her stomach churning.

She noticed a young couple in a vehicle in the opposite lane singing along to the radio and laughing together; it made her smile, thinking that maybe there was hope for her and Donovan. She felt sure that a few words would break his sour mood.

As she turned to him, she noticed that, instead of his usual gentle features, he had a scowl on his face. His eyes appeared vacant, as though he'd switched off. *Maybe he's just lost in his thoughts.* It had been an emotional time. She felt the familiar feeling of anxiety wash over her. 'Where are we going?' she asked.

Donovan ignored her as though he hadn't heard. Again, this time with a quiver in her voice, she said, 'Where are you taking me?'

'Don't ask so many questions,' snapped Donovan. He looked like he had the weight of the world on his shoulders.

'What's going on? I want to know this instant . . . or stop the bloody car and let me out! You're scaring me,' she cried.

'Don't be upset. I've found a solution to our situation. You trust me, don't you?'

'Of course I trust you.' Emily felt foolish, even though she didn't really know what Donovan was talking about. She had trusted him this far, and he had shown her nothing but care and compassion. *Maybe he's just having an off day. He is human.*

After an hour's drive they arrived at a suburb, where the run-down houses had typically been converted into flats; if the occupants opened their window they could practically talk with their neighbours. Emily had no other term for it other than: *a shit hole.*

Donovan stopped the car. 'Grab your bag,' he instructed. Emily's eyes narrowed at Donovan. He just shrugged his shoulders. Following him, she looked around cautiously. The area was rough. She clutched her bag to her chest, almost as a form of protection.

They walked up some steps in the block of flats. The air was filled with the stench of urine and marijuana. Graffiti was written on every wall and litter cluttered the hallways. Emily shuddered as Donovan led her through a doorway into someone's home. *But whose? Surely Donovan doesn't live in a hovel like this?* She kept glancing at Donovan, hoping he'd divulge his reason for taking her there. *What the hell is happening?!*

With only one foot inside the door, she could see two young kids, a boy and a girl. They were trying to escape the cold, huddled under a blanket. The flat was freezing; you could see your breath. The place also needed a good scrub with a bottle of bleach.

Emily's mouth felt dry and she bit her lower lip as she acknowledged how these children—even in this day and age—were living in such squalid conditions. She didn't want to go any further into the flat. Instead, she snapped,

'Goddamn it, Donovan. Who are these kids? Why have you brought me here? Just what is going on?'

It was like they were strangers. He didn't acknowledge her, and she didn't recognise the Donovan stood a few feet away. She reached out and grabbed his arm, saying again, 'What's going on?'

'I'm sorry, Emily. It just has to be this way.'

'What does? I don't understand. What the hell are you talking about?'

'Kids, this is Emily. I've found you a good mother, and from now on, she will take care of you.'

Emily's eyes widened, and her jaw dropped. *What the fuck?!* 'You can't just dump me here! Who are these kids? Are they yours? I demand an explanation!' she shouted, clearly agitated. She rubbed her temples as claustrophobia washed over her. 'And what do you mean 'you've found a mother'?' *Did I hear him properly? Am I losing my mind? If this is a prank, I'm not finding it funny.*

'You'll meet the other three girls later. This is going to be your new home. You can all take care of each other. It's for the best,' said Donovan, avoiding eye contact.

How can he be so callous? Emily stood, rooted to the spot, staring at the two kids with dirt-stained faces, snotty noses and messy hair. *Is this really happening?*

It took Emily just a couple of minutes to realise that trusting in a man was a big mistake. She'd been well and truly stitched up. She finally understood what Donovan was implying.

She wanted to scream. 'I guess you're not staying,' she spat, even though she already knew the answer. 'Look at me!' she yelled. 'Answer my question, dammit.' Shock turned to fury. She raised her arm and swung at Donovan with every ounce of strength she had. Her palm hit his cheek. Her chest pounded as she tried to get her breathing under control.

There was a long pause and the room began to spin for Emily. Bile rose in her throat. Donovan couldn't meet her eyes, and as he headed out the door he didn't look back. 'No, no!' she whispered desperately. *It can't be true . . .* Tears flowed and didn't stop. She hugged herself tightly.

'It's okay, you can stay with us,' said a voice from the comfort of the blanket.

Emily's instinct told her to run out the door, but she couldn't help but feel sorry for the kids. She didn't even know their names, never mind their story.

'Please don't cry,' said the girl with a toothy smile.

From the window of the flat on Clover Road Emily paused, her gut turning inside out. She couldn't go to the police—Donovan was the police. She didn't have any other option, and as she watched Donovan walk to his car without looking back, she saw a hint of Andy in him for a second time. She knew in her heart that she would never see him again.

CHAPTER 43

A few days later, early one morning, Emily sat on a park bench. Her mind floated like the breeze. A takeaway coffee between the palms of her hands, she watched the steam rise, along with her thoughts.

She'd craved freedom for years in some form, and now she had it. Although it wasn't the 'hearts and flowers' ending she'd dreamt about, it was the start of something new. She inhaled the freshness of the frosty morning's air and felt the sting of the chilly wind. She smiled—she felt alive. Never again would she wither and die or cower to someone else's superiority. Freedom felt good.

She'd already come to terms with the fact that she'd been played the fool—truly stitched up by both men in her life. She was glad that her path had led her there and thankful that she was rid of her bastard of a cruel husband. Deep down, dark thoughts lingered. *Have Andy's ways somehow rubbed off on me?* She hoped Andy would suffer and rot in hell, that prison life would bring him pain, torture and molestation. *Maybe an inmate will slit his throat while he sleeps . . . that would be justice.* But, even with Andy locked away, she felt the damage had been done. Memories of him would not be shaken easily. She often heard Andy in her head and felt him on her skin. She saw him in her sleep and lurking around every corner. *Maybe, in time, he'll disappear from my thoughts forever.* She doubted it.

Donovan was cut from a similar cloth; she'd learnt that the hard way. But at least he'd given her freedom and purpose. For the first time in a long time, she recognised herself as something other than weak. Her circumstances, trust and naivety had chained her to five kids in unknown territory, yet the moment she had looked into their eyes she'd caught a glimpse of her own haunted self and she knew exactly what she had to do. She would not abandon them, and neither would she let them fear others.

Emily had encountered loneliness in a cruel world; she felt fortunate that this new life was better than her previous existence. A new beginning was in the making. She'd yearned for it for so long and finally she felt it was attainable. Overnight, she'd become a mother. She didn't know Donovan's agenda for leaving her there nor the kids' story. All she knew was that they needed her as much as she needed them.

She'd felt an instant connection to every one of them. They were kindred spirits—forgotten, lost souls in an unforgiving world.

Emily had learned a hard lesson, but a valuable one nonetheless never would she trust again—there was always a hidden agenda. Never would she crumble in the face of fear either; she vowed to stand and face it. She would never again depend on a guy; she would rather be a happy spinster than an obedient wife. From this point on, she was going to write her own chapter with her ready-made family. She wasn't silly, she knew there would be ups and downs, but she would give it her all. She would instil strength and determination in them, make them independent and give them the skills they needed to forge their own destinies.

She cast her eyes over the park's grounds. She felt a connection: like a weed reaching for the sun through a crack in the pavement, she would blossom and bloom, and no poison would cause her to wither and die.

She smiled as she watched the neighbourhood's fitness freaks racing furiously against the clock. Her past was behind her, her present was in the making, and her future was a whole new adventure.

The End